Montana
Mail Order Brides

A Sweet Historical
Western Romance Series

CHARITY PHILLIPS

MONTANA MAIL ORDER BRIDES
TABLE OF CONTENTS

Montana Mail Order Bride Madeline

Providence, Rhode Island – 1882

The children played merrily in the field, so excited to venture out after a multitude of days stuck inside, escaping the unusually scorching heat of July. Madeline had promised the youngsters a picnic outdoors just as soon as the worst of the heat passed, and today she'd made good on that promise, filling a basket with simple foods for her charges and heading out together into the field behind the house. They skipped through the long grass, skimming their tiny fingers along the tips of the blades.

Suddenly, the scorching heat returned—so hot, it set the blades up ahead afire. Madeline called to the young boy and girl, but her voice came out strangled, muted. She ran toward them, but the faster she moved, the further away they became. The blazing grass raced toward them but the children remained oblivious despite the heat engulfing the field. Panic flooded through every fiber of Madeline's body as she stood there, helpless, powerless; her every effort thwarted by some force conspiring against her.

Madeline awoke abruptly, her heart pounding, sweat dampening her brow; the panic that she had felt in her dream turned to heartache. The children she'd cared for and loved as her own, were gone. She'd left to visit a friend for a few short days, and upon returning, found her entire world had been turned upside down. The family who had taken her in when she'd had no family to call her own had perished in a devastating house fire. She'd been employed as their nanny for three years, and young George, four years old at the time, and his two-year-old sister Charlotte had welcomed her with open arms.

Madeline's lot in life had forced her to be strong and she wasn't easily prone to tears. But the moment she discovered her young charges' lives had ended so suddenly, so tragically, tears streamed down her cheeks. She'd stood silent in front of the burnt ruins for so long, her legs had grown numb from their burden. She couldn't force herself to leave, frozen, somehow waiting for her bleary eyes to clear and find the house standing in all its prior glory, and George and Charlotte running out the front door to greet her. Finally, as night had begun to fall, some neighbor took her by the shoulders, guiding her away from the mound of ashes and rubble.

The next several days passed by in a blur, Madeline still too much in shock to move forward. Eventually, she found temporary lodging and then work as a housekeeper, knowing her meager savings wouldn't sustain her for long. She had tried to pick up the pieces of her life in the weeks that had followed her return to Providence, but normality, peace, were nowhere to be found. She saw George and Charlotte everywhere and in everything she did. Just yesterday, she had woken late, and out of habit, rushed out of bed to fix the youngsters breakfast. Coming awake as she hurried, Madeline had stopped herself mid-step, remembering that she was not in the home she'd known for years nor were her children there waiting anxiously to bid her good morning. And later, rifling through her only suitcase of belongings, she came across the book she'd been reading to the children the night before she'd left; she'd tossed the book across the room in frustration. "I should have finished the book with them," she thought irrationally, as if having done so would have assuaged the pain somehow.

Sitting at the small table now with her breakfast growing colder by the minute, she browsed through the Providence Daily Post, looking for something that might occupy her thoughts, even for a few moments. But, the news was disturbing—or dull at best—nothing there to distract her from her sorrow. Opting to turn one more page before abandoning her effort, something caught her eye: men from Montana, looking for brides to join them there. It wasn't anything she would have ever considered before. In truth, the matter of men and women, complete strangers, coming together in matrimony to better one's position, to procreate advantageously; it all seemed too absurd to Madeline. If she ever married, she'd been determined that it would be for love and nothing else. Not that the prospect had ever been very likely. Sure, Madeline was beautiful—long, fiery tresses, vivid emerald eyes, a thin, feminine frame—but she was also a near-penniless orphan who, until recently, kept company with children.

But now, the prospect of escaping Providence to some foreign place with no memories to haunt her at every turn, it seemed worth abandoning her prior determination. It couldn't hurt to take a look, she thought. And so, she read through the column of advertisements filled with men seeking women for marriage, rolling her eyes as each one sounded nearly identical to the next:

"A bachelor of 48 seeks a wife. She must be under thirty years of age, amiable and well-versed in maintaining a home," the advertisements read.

Of course. Every old farmer there wants a young, attractive woman to do his bidding and keep his house clean, she thought dryly, finding less and less appeal in the prospect. And then she came across one advertisement that captured her interest:

"A bachelor of 32 years seeks an intelligent, amiable wife to join him in Montana."

It wasn't very often she'd heard of a man in search of an intelligent woman, and it certainly made him stand out. And so, on a whim, she responded to his advertisement, writing him a letter—an honest letter—about herself. Madeline saw no benefit in exaggerating the truth or hiding the dirty laundry; she'd rather him reject her now than after she'd gone and moved across the country. She did, however, make her urgency clear, wanting to be away from Providence as soon as possible. Before she could change her mind, she sent the letter off and endeavored not to think of it again. After all, it would be weeks before she received a response, if the man was even interested.

But as the weeks passed, Madeline thought about the man from Montana a great deal; every time Providence haunted her, she longed for the escape. A time or two she'd even wished she'd elaborated a little in her correspondence, making it more likely she could hope for a response. So, four weeks later, when she'd all but given up, it came as quite a surprise to find a letter addressed to her, posted from Montana. She'd learned about how these things worked a little during the past few weeks; lengthy written exchanges back and forth, each party taking their

4

time in determining whether the match was a good fit. And so, it came as an even greater surprise to find a brief note from the man in Montana, along with a train ticket:

> Please join me in Montana. I have made travel arrangements for you, and expect that we can deal with the matter of matrimony upon your arrival.
> Sincerely,
> Adam Black

He isn't exactly the chatty type, is he? Madeline thought, but it didn't matter; she held her key to escape in her hands. In just a few short days, she could leave Providence and, hopefully, leave behind some of the heartache that the city held for her now. For the first time in so many weeks, she smiled, darting around her tiny lodging, collecting her few belongings and tidying the room. In just twenty minutes, she was packed and ready to leave...with three days to spare. "Arghhh!" she fumed aloud, wanting to be on her way already, but she could be patient just a little longer.

Madeline spent the remaining days saying goodbye to the place she'd called home for her entire twenty years, and on the last day, visited the burnt down home she'd avoided all these weeks. She wandered around the mound of rubble to the field behind where she'd spent so many hours with her charges, playing games, reading stories. She could see each scene so vividly that she almost reached out to touch the characters playing in her imagination. "Goodbye, my dear George. Farewell, sweet Charlotte," she said simply instead, a lonesome tear escaping as she turned away, walking back to the road and away from that sad chapter of her life forever.

****

The sun rose early in the sky, and Madeline was already awake, tidying her small space for the last time. Her suitcase sat near the door and her eyes kept darting to it, waiting for the moment it would be time to leave. She couldn't remember ever being so anxious for something in her life, and given that she was leaving to some great unknown, it surprised her that she wasn't more fearful of her coming adventure. But even as she closed the door behind her for the last time, carrying her small suitcase down the stairs to the street below, she didn't suffer a moment of trepidation. Regardless of what Montana held in store, it could be no worse than remaining in Providence.

She stepped onto the train an hour later feeling no less confident, but Mr. Black surprised her once again. As she handed her ticket to the conductor, his eyes widened briefly before offering his arm to lead her through the cars as he signaled another man to carry Madeline's luggage behind them. They passed by a multitude of passengers and empty seats along the way, making Madeline weary that perhaps the conductor intended to walk her right back off the train, but a moment later, he brought them to a halt as he opened the door to an empty car. She surveyed her surroundings, impressed by the spacious and comfortable looking area in front of her. Looking up at the conductor quizzically, he motioned for her to step inside, holding the door and then entering behind her.

"I hope you'll find everything satisfactory, Miss. Please let me know if you have any need of my service while you are aboard," he finished, nodding his head in a curt bow before leaving through the same door they had entered.

The man with her suitcase placed it gently on the ground, nodding before leaving as well. "Sir, wait," she started. "Is there some reason I've been sequestered here?" she asked, not certain why she'd been deposited into an empty train car.

The baggage man gave her a curious look. "The car has been reserved for your use alone, Miss, but of course you are free to come and go as you please." He smiled kindly before heading back out into the preceding car.

There must have been thirty or more passengers on each of the cars they'd traveled through, and here she was with an entire car all to herself. What had Mr. Black been thinking? Had he intended to sway her with an impressive show of wealth? Her decision would had to have been made already before boarding the train, so it could not have helped to sway her. Did he not know that? Wonderful, I've chosen marriage to an idiot, she thought silently, and then immediately felt guilty for presuming to judge the man's character so quickly; so Madeline took a seat, relaxing in the privacy of her very own train car, determined to enjoy the trip.

Her excitement rose as she felt the train begin to pull out of the station. There was no turning back now. She watched out the window as Providence became nothing but a blur in the background, and determinedly turned her thoughts to what lay up ahead. She'd read about Montana and the other Western territories briefly; largely inhabited by farmers, miners and prospectors, there was a definite shortage of eligible ladies suitable for marriage. Funny that it hadn't occurred to Madeline to research more about her prospective new home when she'd sent the letter to Mr. Black, but she never put much weight in receiving a response, so the task seemed unnecessary. Besides, a brand new adventure in a foreign place wasn't the worst thing in the world.

Madeline spent the remainder of the trip thinking

about what her new life may have in store for her. At first, she'd presumed Mr. Black would be a struggling farmer or miner, but it seemed unlikely that a struggling man in any trade wouldn't have been able to secure an entire passenger car for a virtual stranger. Perhaps he'd been there long enough that he'd become rather prosperous. Or maybe he was already wealthy and he'd headed out west in search of something new. She wasn't sure why, but that notion excited Madeline and heightened her interest in meeting Mr. Black. The prospect of an exciting and adventurous husband certainly held more appeal than the straight-laced, boring sort of men she'd had the opportunity to become acquainted with thus far in her short life.

****

Her musings kept her so occupied over the next several days that Madeline hardly noticed time going by, and before she knew it, the train was pulling into the station in Helena, Montana. For the first time, she felt nervousness course through her body as she stood at the door of the train car, willing her legs to propel her forward. Finally, her determination won out and she stepped off the train, her eyes surveying the crowd. She realized she had no idea how she would identify Mr. Black, nor how he would recognize a woman he'd never seen.

Her attention was momentarily drawn elsewhere; a particularly handsome man stood out to her from among the rest. He was tall, standing at least half a foot above Madeline's tall frame. His dark hair was cropped short, and his crystal clear, blue eyes were the most remarkable eyes she'd ever seen. His suit had to be expensive and the man wearing it was obviously fit, his broad chest and muscular build obvious even through the impeccable clothing. He turned and his eyes found her, meeting her gaze unwaveringly, and then he started toward her. Madeline's brow furrowed in confusion; she knew many men in Montana were desperate for wives, and perhaps this one had decided he'd sweet talk a woman right off the train. Indignation welled within her, but Madeline did her best to rein it in, figuring it would be indecent to make a scene in the middle of the train station. The man continued toward her, stopping less than two feet from where she stood.

"Good afternoon, Miss Swan. My name is Adam Black," he began, smiling at her politely and instantly lightening his previously unreadable expression. "And now, I believe we have been formally introduced."

She nodded, thrown to discover that the incredibly

handsome man was in fact the man she'd come here to marry.

"Good afternoon, Mr. Black," she replied cordially, finding her voice.

"If you'll come with me, I'd be happy to escort you to your new home while we take the opportunity to get acquainted." He offered his arm and she took it without question. Her mind was busily absorbed trying to figure out Mr. Black: He is obviously wealthy, and definitely attractive; what need did he have to seek out a woman in this way? she wondered.

"You have questions," he stated as they walked away from the station, reading her silence perfectly.

"I apologize for being so forward, Mr. Black, but I admit I'm quite confused. You are certainly not what I had expected. A struggling farmer or miner of average looks and intelligence, perhaps. But already it seems unlikely that you have had troubles finding a potential wife," she confessed as they approached an impressive-looking horse-drawn carriage. A man there opened the door and Adam helped Madeline inside. Once seated, he looked at her silently, as if he were contemplating his next words. She sat quietly as the carriage began to move, waiting.

"I suppose I should be up front with you, Miss Swan, as you were with me in your letter," he sighed. "It is true that I have had marriage prospects aplenty—my father ensures a steady stream of them, desperate to see his eldest son settled in the confines of matrimony, but, even had I been inclined to take a bride, those simple-minded girls would have driven me mad; all clamoring to climb the ranks of society, even if they must relegate themselves to surviving halfway across the country. Even more, a woman who enters into marriage in the usual way expects a certain degree of...fidelity, and I have yet to find a woman who could occupy my thoughts for long. So, you see, this arrangement of ours is an ideal situation: you have escaped your prior home to an elevated status in a new place, and I have satisfied my father's desire for his son to settle down," he finished.

Madeline was quiet for a moment, processing this new information. No part of this had gone as she had expected. "So, in truth, it is not a marriage you are seeking, but rather a union on paper to satisfy your father?" she asked, though it was more a statement, reviewing her thoughts aloud, rather than a question. And then another thought came to her, "A marriage to a poor orphan; will that not irk your father more than satisfy him?"

Adam smiled devilishly and Madeline's heart skipped a beat. No wonder he had no interest in settling down; this man could make any woman swoon with a smile like that.

"My father may not have anticipated my particular choice, but I believe it is suffice to say that I don't feel it is any of his concern," Adam finished curtly, though the defiant light in his eyes told Madeline he was more than pleased by the turn of events.

She wasn't sure she was comfortable with this arrangement at all, but what choice did she have now? She'd traveled all this way and had nowhere to go, even if she could afford to travel back to Providence. At least she knew what to expect.

****

The rest of the ride continued in silence. Madeline wasn't sure she wanted to pry anymore, and it seemed Mr. Black was giving her an opportunity to digest the new information he'd shared. He sat forward as they neared a large stretch of land with a house set back from the dusty road. Her gaze followed his out the window and it was all she could do to keep her jaw from dropping open, seeing the enormous, whitewashed house up ahead. The home seemed almost out of place when compared to the homesteads they'd passed on their way; it was at least twice, maybe three times the size of the family's home she'd lived in back in Providence, and the grounds out front were immaculate.

"Welcome to your new home, Miss Swan," Adam turned to her, his eyes narrowing as if he were trying to read her response. What he found seemed to please him because his lips turned up in a comfortable smile.

"It's beautiful," she breathed, now close enough to see the intricate detail in every inch of woodwork covering the grand building.

And then his expression changed, irritation flashing across his features as he spotted a carriage up ahead. "Forgive me, Miss Swan. I've been away from my home for the past several days and had expected this particular trouble to have been gone by now," he told her cryptically.

Madeline's gaze followed his to the carriage in front of the house, trying to figure out how its presence could have darkened his mood so suddenly, but the reason became quite clear a moment later as their driver stopped next to the carriage, coming around to open their door. Adam descended first, hesitantly offering her his hand.

"Brace yourself," he warned her as she climbed down, turning to see two women walking out of the house and heading toward them.

Both women were attractive, one substantially older than the other. The younger looked similar in age to Madeline, but the way she carried herself made it clear that she was most definitely from the upper class.

"Good afternoon, Mr. Black," the elder woman greeted Adam, stopping a foot or two in front of them.

"Good afternoon, Mrs. Brady," Adam replied, a tolerant look on his face. "I hadn't expected the continued pleasure of your company." Though his words were cordial, the undertones of sarcasm were evident.

The woman ignored Madeline altogether at first, but eventually her curiosity got the better of her and her eyes shifted, looking Madeline up and down like she were some odd creature.

"And who is this you've brought with you?" Mrs. Brady inquired.

The woman didn't sound the least bit happy, so much so that Madeline was surprised she had been described as a 'who' rather than a 'what.'

Adam turned to Madeline with a question in his eyes. She had no idea how, but somehow, she knew precisely what question he was asking. While she was not the least bit settled with his particular matrimonial arrangement, she'd come all this way and it seemed to her she had very few other options. She nodded almost imperceptibly, but it was enough to answer Adam's question.

"May I present to you Mrs. Brady, my betrothed, Miss Madeline Swan," he spoke regally, and Madeline could see the impish light dancing in his crystal blue eyes once again.

Given that Mrs. Brady didn't appear to be a kind or decent person, Madeline couldn't help but smile at the delight Adam was taking in irking the woman. She was silent for a moment, stunned by his announcement, no doubt.

"I see," she replied, finding her voice a moment later. "Margaret and I were about to have tea in the parlor. Would you care to join us?" she offered cordially while her eyes shot daggers at Madeline.

"I apologize ladies, but you will have to begin without us. Madeline and I have both traveled quite a distance and I would like to give her an opportunity to get settled before...entertaining," he finished, his last word likely a cover for what would really have taken place in the parlor should Mrs. Brady be let loose on Madeline.

"Good day, Mrs. Brady, Margaret," he nodded to each of the women and then guided Madeline up the stairs and into the house.

It seemed Madeline hadn't been at her new home five minutes and already she'd managed to make an enemy, but once behind closed doors, she did her best to shake off the uncomfortable encounter outside and instead turn her attention to Adam and her new home. It certainly was magnificent; intricate detail throughout—the finest of furniture and lively colors everywhere she looked—but it was so large, she worried she might get lost in the house should she be left to find her way around alone.

"I'll escort you to your room, Miss Swan," Adam told her, leading her toward the massive staircase winding up to the second floor of the home.

She nodded, following behind him. She stopped to admire the railing's woodwork; although she didn't know much about the craft, her father had been an enthusiast. While her family never had a great deal of money when she was a child, her father had taken the time to lovingly carve every piece of furniture and every piece of wood that graced their small home. Now seeing the intricacy of the work in this house, she could vividly envision the effort and care clearly.

Adam didn't seem to mind her dawdling, waiting patiently for Madeline to resume her ascent up the stairs. He led her down the long hall to the second door from the end; what she found inside was no less breathtaking than the rest of the house, exquisitely furnished and so large she wondered if the quarters had been meant for an entire family.

"I'll leave you to change and freshen up. Would you join me for tea in, let's say, an hour?" he asked.

Feeling the weight of just how poor she was, Madeline blushed lightly. "I'm afraid I'm as freshened up as I can be, Mr. Black. The clothes you see are the finest I own." She forced her voice to remain steady, just shy of proud, despite the embarrassment roiling within her.

He was silent for a moment, his eyes searching for something in her expression yet again. And then he nodded as if finalizing some decision. "I will have someone here to fit you for a wardrobe tomorrow. Until then, you'll find my mother's clothing in the closet by the bed. She was about your size. Please feel free to make your selection from there."

"Oh no, I couldn't possibly," Madeline began, not the least bit comfortable with taking his mother's clothes or accepting his offer.

"Of course you could. You will soon be my wife and so it is my responsibility to see that you're adequately attired," he stated matter-of-factly.

"That's not necessary," Madeline assured him. She wasn't comfortable taking handouts, regardless of what duty compelled the giver. "I'm sure I can find work to support myself, Mr. Black," she affirmed, fire in her eyes, blazing against the notion of being the recipient of charity or pity.

"I find it unlikely you'll find the type of work to which you're accustomed...nor morally bound to reject," he replied, though a very different type of fire seemed to be setting his crystal eyes ablaze. And that fiery gaze seemed to be doing strange things to Madeline, making her heart beat faster while an odd warmth spread throughout her body. The sensation was so foreign that Madeline just wanted the exchange to end. She needed time to analyze whatever this strange new feeling was—without Mr. Black's crystal fire muddling her thoughts.

"I will consider your offer. Thank you, Mr. Black," she spoke suddenly and then waited expectedly for him to leave.

He smiled, a knowing expression on his face, and then bowed curtly before making his exit. Once alone, Madeline wandered around the room, breathing deeply to regain her composure. Trying to be rational, she opened the closet door, peering in at an enormous selection of stunning dresses. There were so many, she wondered if the woman had ever worn the same dress twice! One dress in particular caught Madeline's eye. It wasn't at all the most intricate or expensive garment in the collection, but it was simply beautiful. She ran her fingers along the soft, cream-colored fabric and lifted it from the rack.

"It couldn't hurt to try it on," she reasoned aloud, sliding off her travel-weary attire and slipping into the gown.

She took the time to thoroughly comb through her long tresses—something her previous schedule seldom allowed. She tied her silken hair atop her head in a simple knot and surveyed the results in the gilded mirror resting against the wall. If Madeline had been a beauty in her common clothes with her hair pulled back quickly and sternly, she was absolutely stunning now with red tendrils of hair cascading from the loose knot, gently framing her feminine features and drawing attention to her unusually vivid green eyes.

Checking the clock, she realized she still had some time to spare. She sat down, perched at the edge of the seat and waited. She'd investigated the room and felt too uncomfortable to venture out to explore the house on her own. Her thoughts returned to Adam's expectations for their impending marriage. She had never considered the possibility that she would be wed to a man who had no interest in their marriage whatsoever. Would they remain strangers living in the same home? Maintain separate rooms? Come together only for the purpose of public appearances? And what about children?

It was far too much for Madeline to sort through at the moment, and so she pushed the thoughts away. She'd give herself an opportunity to become acquainted with her new home and her new life before worrying about the rest.

****

Five minutes later, there was a knock at the door. She stood, fiddling with the dress she wasn't entirely certain she should be wearing, and called for the knocker to enter. Adam opened the door and moved to enter, his gaze searching for her in the enormous room. He stopped abruptly, his eyes finding her, and he was speechless. He stared at her for a moment and Madeline grew uncomfortable under his gaze.

"I'm sorry, Mr. Black. I had only meant to take a look; I hadn't intended to take you up on your offer. All of the dresses were exquisite, of course, but when I saw this one in particular, well, I couldn't resist," she stumbled through an explanation.

"It's quite alright, Madeline." Her eyes flew up when he addressed her by her first name. "You just caught me off-guard, that's all. You look beautiful, to say the least. The most beautiful woman I've ever seen, in fact."

"Oh, thank you," she acknowledged uncomfortably, while the strange warmth coursed through her body anew in response to his heated gaze.

He offered his arm and she accepted, her arm tingling where it made contact with his skin. They descended the stairs and Adam led them to the parlor and Madeline held her breath, hoping desperately that the two women she'd met earlier had vacated the room already. She breathed a sigh of relief, finding the room empty, and sat down in one of the cozy chairs situated next to an enormous hearth.

Adam told her about the area as she sipped on her tea, and she could so easily read his emotion in his expression. By the time he was finished, she knew precisely what excited him about this distant land—the unknown, the adventure.

She told him more about her life in Providence, finding

him a strangely easy conversation partner. She'd never conversed so easily with anyone in her life. As she came to the tragedy that had forever changed the course of her life, Madeline swallowed hard against the emotion caught in her throat and tears welling in her eyes.

"I'm sorry. As you can see, I haven't yet fully recovered," she apologized for her emotional display.

Adam reached across the distance between them to place his hand on her knee, earnest sympathy in his eyes. But it was at that exact moment that Mrs. Brady and her daughter Margaret chose to make their entrance into the parlor.

"It seems you and your young bride are in need of a chaperone, Mr. Black." The words were spoken lightly enough, but the undertones in her voice conveyed her displeasure at the scene adequately.

"I believe I have long outgrown the need of a chaperone, Mrs. Brady—and, frankly, I don't believe it is your place to dictate such things in my home."

Seeing no way to persist in her original course, Mrs. Brady changed the subject, directing attention elsewhere. "Isn't that your mother's favorite dress? The poor woman would turn over in her grave to find you doling out her prized possessions."

Madeline paled. By the way Adam had spoken about his mother's clothes, she'd just assumed that she was back home with his father in the east. Her eyes flew to Adam, and she was about to apologize profusely when he spoke up instead.

"Quite the opposite, I'm sure. I am certain that my mother would be delighted to find her beautiful daughter-in-law is keeping her favorite items from wasting away in her closet."

That seemed to silence Mrs. Brady temporarily, but it

wasn't long before she started along a new line of questioning.

"Tell me, how exactly did you and Miss Swan meet? It seems that just a month ago, you were set in your bachelor ways, and suddenly, you've decided to take a bride. This young thing isn't with child, is she?"

Adam's eyes flared with anger and he removed his hand from Madeline's knee. She watched his hands curl into fists as he gritted his teeth, obviously working to keep himself in check. He stood slowly, turning to address the brash woman. Mrs. Brady seemed to recognize the error of her ways immediately, a look of distress on her face.

"Miss Swan has already proven herself far more civilized than you, biting her tongue as you seek to make her uncomfortable in her own home," he uttered seethingly. "I, on the other hand, have had my fill of your rudeness this afternoon. I believe it is time for you and your daughter to make your return home. And you can inform my father that he has no more need to send desperate young ladies and their mothers to the west in pursuit of my vast fortune."

Mrs. Brady's entire face had turned crimson with embarrassment. Madeline couldn't help but to feel a little sorry for the woman, so determined to marry off her daughter into money that she'd make a fool of herself to do so. Mother and daughter were speechless as they left the parlor, and Adam took a seat moment later, looking fully composed already.

"Why did you choose me?"

The question slipped out of Madeline's mouth unbidden. She hadn't intended to broach the subject until she'd had the opportunity to sort through her own feelings about their present arrangement.

"In truth, it was quite simple. You wanted to get away

from Providence quickly; you weren't interested in learning about what type of life I could provide or whether I would elevate your status in society. Whatever your reasons, they could not be so devious in nature," he responded easily. "And why, may I ask, did you respond to my advertisement in particular?"

"All of the others wanted a pretty, young thing with no wits about them," she replied simply. "There was no potential for a relationship to develop there. With you, I had thought—"

"That we would meet and fall madly in love?" he asked gently. "I have seen it once or twice, Madeline, but in truth, most love is a fairy tale made up by young children. If ever it exists, it inevitably ends in hatred or heartache. This is far better, this amicable arrangement we've made."

She nodded, seeing no point in pursuing an argument over this matter. It was obvious Adam's mind was most certainly made up. And so she rose, pleading tiredness after her lengthy trip.

"Please, don't trouble yourself. Surely, I can find my way back," she told him as he moved to escort her there. Adam nodded curtly and Madeline headed upstairs to her rooms. She'd made up the excuse that she was tired from her travels, but as she sprawled out on the bed, exhaustion overtook her quickly. Before she could object to her first mid-day nap since childhood, her heavy eyes closed and she was fast asleep.

****

She awoke sometime later, an image of Adam Black at the forefront of her mind, having carried it forward from the dream that had occupied her mind while she slept. She couldn't recall the particulars, but his blue eyes stood out to her, blazing with crystal fire in the same way they had when he'd looked at her earlier that day. And then she noticed light shining in through the window; that was the morning sun, she was sure of it. She'd slept fully through the rest of the day and the night without awaking once. While she worried the household would now believe her to be a lazy sloth, it amazed her that she'd slept so long. She hadn't gotten a good night's sleep since the day she'd returned to Providence, and here she was now, more than fully rested. Although their arrangement was not what she had expected, it may have truly been a good choice.

And with that knowledge, Madeline decided it was time to begin her new life here. She readied herself and rushed down the stairs, hoping she wasn't too late for breakfast. She moved so quickly that she nearly knocked Adam over, running into him in the foyer at the bottom of the stairs. Her hands made contact with his broad chest to steady herself, stunned briefly by their unexpected collision. She looked up at him and in that moment, she wanted to kiss him, to feel the gentle touch of his lips pressed against hers. Madeline! she chided herself sternly, flabbergasted by the improper thought. She pulled her hands away quickly, apologizing for her haste.

"It's alright. I get quite excited over breakfast, too," he teased. "But I promise the cook will keep it warm for us."

"Well then, I suppose I can take my time," she recanted good-naturedly, happy that he'd lightened the mood so easily.

They continued to the dining room together and

Madeline was relieved to discover there were no unfriendly guests joining them this morning.

"I'm afraid Mrs. Brady and her daughter had to be on their way home," he'd told her with that impish light in his eyes again. She'd just nodded, trying to resist a smile.

Breakfast was scrumptious and the conversation was pleasant. Madeline was still surprised by how easily she could talk to Adam and just how at ease he seemed to be when conversing with her. It was like they were old souls, already well-acquainted somehow. The following weeks progressed in a similar manner, sharing meals together, touring the grounds surrounding the house, and even making the occasional trip into town.

The more she learned about Adam, the more highly she regarded him. Even though he'd been born into money, he'd never settled for an easy life, opting instead to see what he could accomplish on his own. And he'd been extremely successful, first in farming and then in finding a few choice spots to establish a small mining operation. All of the men who worked for Adam were paid well and the work that was expected of them was always reasonable. He didn't believe in taking advantage of others for his own benefit.

Unfortunately, it wasn't only a high regard she'd developed for Adam. He was kind, considerate, thoughtful, and yet strong and intelligent; it would be impossible for any woman living in such close proximity to the man not to develop deep feelings for him. But because there was nothing she could do about it, Madeline had no choice but to try burying her feelings.

And then one evening, discord suddenly filled their superficial relationship. Adam had come home after venturing out late—Madeline didn't even want to guess at where he had been going. He'd walked back in the front door not a full hour later as she had sat reading in the parlor. Adam had stormed into the room, standing at the door and glaring at her without saying a word. She'd waited for him to speak but it seemed like the silence would continue indefinitely. She was just about to turn her attention back to her book when he started; his voice angry, frustrated.

"This was not supposed to happen. This was supposed to be convenient. Ha! It isn't convenient; it's quite unsettling, to say the least," he exclaimed, pacing the room while rubbing his forehead. "And what am I to do now? You see, I don't want them, Madeline; they now hold about as much appeal as an old mare. It seems you've spoiled me!"

He started into the room, taking no more than three steps in her direction before stopping abruptly. His expression was fraught with indecision as he stared at her, but a moment later, he turned around and headed back out the door, thundering up the stairs to his room. She knew he'd reached his destination by the loud thud of the door closing behind him.

She sat there more confused than ever before with absolutely no idea of what he'd been rambling on about. She'd never seen him like that; perhaps he'd gotten drunk and was spewing nonsense in his stupor, but it seemed rather out of character for the Adam she'd come to know over the past weeks.

He returned to the parlor about an hour later, moving more slowly now. The anger was gone, but still he somehow didn't seem himself.

"You recover quickly," Madeline said, giggling suddenly, then unable to help herself. The tumultuous emotions of the past hours seemed to have gotten the best of her at that moment.

Adam just looked at her, no doubt concerned over her state of mind given her sudden outburst.

"I'm sorry, Mr. Black. It has just been a very unusual day," she continued to smile as she spoke. "I believe that when you have the choice between tears and laughter, choose laughter. It is the best medicine, after all," she added, trying to reassure him that she was in fact sane.

She watched as sadness flashed briefly through his eyes, so quickly that she may not have noticed had she not been observing his expression intently.

"What's wrong?" Madeline asked, his perplexity growing by the minute over their strange exchange this evening.

"That is precisely what my mother used to say," he replied. "I can tell already that you are so much like her."

The words sounded like a compliment, but the unsettled expression he wore confused her.

"She was the kind of woman who loved with every fiber of her being, and I can see that in you, Madeline. She could never have been satisfied with a life like this," he finished sadly.

She rose, moving to stand in front of Adam. "This arrangement is not precisely what I had expected, but is that your concern? Do you think I'm unhappy? You have taken me away from heartache and given me a beautiful home in a wonderful new place. And you've become...a good friend," she answered, pausing briefly to figure out how best to understate her feelings while reassuring him that she did not regret her choice.

He nodded, moving to touch her cheek with the palm of his hand, igniting the warm, tingling sensation she felt whenever he had touched her. She didn't say a word as Adam leaned in; she'd longed for him to kiss her and it was finally going to happen. He hovered just an inch or two away—and had Madeline been bolder, she might have crossed the distance between them—but she remained still, waiting with an overwhelming sense of anticipation. Suddenly, Adam turned away, walking out of the room once again without a word.

Standing alone in the parlor, it was Madeline's turn to feel frustration. She'd thought that perhaps something had changed his mind; that he'd come to realize the hollowness in his marriage arrangement.

Then it dawned on her; perhaps Adam had simply been unable to find a woman to satisfy his baser needs this night. He'd come to her, not as a man with desire for his intended wife, but as a man with no other options. And even then, he'd walked away, making it abundantly clear that he would not be swayed, even in desperation.

She left the parlor a moment later, after being sure Adam had plenty of time to return to his room, not wanting to run into him yet again this evening. Once in her room, she curled up in the center of her enormous bed. She felt alone in a way she had never known before, never needing the warm arms of a man around her. He'd gone ahead and set the date; in just a week's time she would be wed, and what she would give to truly be his wife. Madeline drifted off to sleep, her mind absorbed with thoughts of Adam and what could have been, had he not been so determined to maintain his distance from her.

****

When she awoke in the morning, those images still vivid in her mind, she couldn't resist bringing up the issue just one more time. Adam was a reasonable man; he had to be able to see what a fine marriage they could make. She readied herself for breakfast and descended the grand staircase, feeling full of hope for their future, but as she entered the dining room, her plans were dashed quickly. Adam had left for several days, the house staff had informed her. He wasn't expected to return until the eve of their upcoming nuptials.

"Well, so much for that plan," Madeline thought, feeling rather deflated. It wasn't that she couldn't speak with him upon his return, but somehow everyday closer to her wedding day seemed to further solidify the cold deal. He had made his intentions clear from the start, hadn't he? What did it matter that she loved him? Her love was unnecessary, unwelcome in a loveless marriage.

Love?!? Her eyes flew wide open, never having put a name to her feelings before. "No, this can't be. I do not love Adam Black," she spoke aloud like a petulant child—but, of course, she did.

It all suddenly made sense. She had thought she'd escaped Providence scot-free; that the fates had finally smiled upon her, or taken pity on her sad situation, but it was clear now that nothing was without a cost. The payment she would make for escaping her former life was to live with the man she loved, never having the feeling returned. He would go about his life and his dalliances, and she would watch helplessly from close proximity. The knowledge seemed to drain her, making Madeline feel like she hadn't slept in days.

She drifted through the next few days. As much as she didn't want to, she couldn't help but look forward to

Adam's return. She'd come to enjoy their conversations very much and couldn't wait for them to resume.

****

The eve of her wedding had finally arrived, and while she felt no particular anticipation over the following day, she peered out the window at least a dozen times waiting for Adam to arrive home.

It was well into the afternoon when his carriage stopped in front of the house. She didn't wait to see him exit the carriage, but instead hurried down the stairs, composing herself once she reached the bottom. She had nearly reached the door when it opened from outside, but it was not Adam who first entered the house.

"Oh dear," she thought silently. Though she'd never seen him before, the man looked like a near replica of Adam, but with thirty or so years between them. This was his father—the one Adam had delighted in irking with his choice in marriage. She wondered if he would be even more brutal than Mrs. Brady had been.

"Father, may I present to you Miss Madeline Swan," Adam announced as he entered behind his father, moving to stand next to her.

His father was silent for a moment, and Madeline tried to mentally prepare herself for whatever blow the man had in store. He looked at her intently, reading her expression in the same way his son had done numerous times before.

At least I know where he gets it from, she thought wryly.

The scene at the front door remained like a frozen tableau for what seemed like an eternity, though in reality it was likely not more than a few moments' time.

"It's a pleasure to meet you, Miss Swan," he began, far more cordially than Madeline had expected. "I do believe Adam was right: the way you hold yourself, the look in your eyes, so very much like my late wife. I must presume then that everything else he has said about you is true as well," the man smiled brightly. "I believe this union will be an ideal match for my son, and so I welcome you to our family."

"Thank you, Mr. Black. It is my honor," Madeline replied shakily, having expected a very different response. She released the breath she hadn't realized she'd been holding.

"And now, I'm going to see about having my belongings brought in safely," he smiled again and returned outside onto the porch.

"Marry me, Madeline Swan," Adam spoke, turning to look at her and take her hands in his.

Madeline looked up at him, puzzled. Wasn't this deal already made?

"Be my wife, not merely in name, but in truth," he began to explain as Madeline's eyes flew open wide yet again.

"I had to leave these past few days, you see. You were driving me mad. You are beautiful, kind, gentle, intelligent; all that a man could want in a wife, but as you know, I thought that love was not what I wanted. I am here to tell you now that I was wrong, Madeline. I don't know precisely how or when it happened, but I have fallen in love with you, and it is you with whom I want to share my life... to bear my children," he continued, gazing at her with loving eyes.

"Mr. Black, you cannot talk me into modifying our arrangement," she began, pausing for effect, but given the unhappy look on Adam's face, she was quick to continue.

"You cannot talk me into it because... I love you, too. There is no convincing necessary," she confessed.

He smiled brightly and his arms pulled her against him as his lips descended upon hers, kissing her with a fervor she could never have imagined. Adam's father returned then, coming to halt inside the door and clearing his throat to announce his presence.

"Don't you think you're acting a little preemptively, son? I do believe the wedding is not until tomorrow," he spoke sternly, but Madeline could see the light dancing in his eyes.

The next day, the two were wed in a small, but beautiful ceremony in the courtyard of their home. Madeline looked stunning in her flowing white gown and had never imagined she could be any happier than she had been that day, but through the years, she was blessed with a loving marriage and a family that delighted her more and more every day. Though Madeline had never been one to believe in fairy tales, she couldn't deny that the fates seemed to have surprised her with her very own happily ever after.

THE END

Montana Mail Order Bride Clara

New York City, 1890

It was a quiet funeral service. Only a few dear old friends, most of them close to the grave themselves, were gathered around the gravesite. They watched in somber silence as dirt was tossed onto the already lowered casket. Clara stood nearest the edge clutching at the thorny stem of a single rose. It was white and delicate, not unlike Clara herself. It was difficult for her to hold without crumpling, her crutches making her stance awkward and her hands constantly full. Her legs were weak, unfortunately, and Clara knew better than to attempt standing without them. As the grave diggers continued to shovel the damp dirt into her grandmother's grave, Clara took a steadying breath before managing to toss the rose in to mix with it.

Clara stayed until it was filled, though everyone else had already left. They had murmured soft condolences and patted her gently on the shoulder, telling her what a shame it was and how great a woman her grandmother had been. By the time it was only Clara and the grave diggers, she finally allowed herself to cry messily. Tears streamed freely down her face as she acknowledged her true, deep shame.

She was relieved.

Her grandmother had been sick for the last three years of Clara's life. It was a terrible, debilitating disease that had left her grandmother mostly bedridden. On occasion, Clara had managed to go outside with her grandmother, but it had been difficult. Between her own disability and her grandmother's illness, neither of the women had fared well.

Being the only living relative of her poor old grandmother, Clara had been dutiful until the end. But it had cost her. What feeble life she had built after her terrible horse riding accident had disintegrated the moment her grandmother had required constant care. Her work had suffered, too, though not nearly as badly. As a secretary, her job was mainly to write down important memos, but even that had become impossible when her grandmother could no longer be left alone.

When the rain started to fall, the grave diggers had already left and Clara was standing alone. Leaning awkwardly on her left crutch, Clara managed to wipe at her face, smearing away at least some of her tears. With a shuddering breath, Clara turned away from her grandmother's final resting place and began the slow walk out of the cemetery.

She hobbled down the gentle slope, reaching the gates and passing through them. The rain had started in earnest now and her black dress was quickly becoming soaked. Mud already lined the edges of her full skirt, making the already heavy material weigh on her.

She hailed a hackman, grateful for the quick single horse carriage as opposed to the clunky double horse taxi, which was far more expensive. He pulled the horse to a stop beside her, careful to not allow his cab wheel to splash a puddle on her.

"Ma'am, where to?"

"The Windermere on West 57th," Clara told the hackman.

He nodded, then took a closer look at her. Clara was prepared for the sudden shift in expression to a mixture of pity and disgust, but she had never cared for it. After six years of her life spent with these leg braces, she had learned to ignore people's ill ease in regards to them, but that didn't make her like it.

After a moment, the hackman hopped down from his coach perch and quickly came around to the door. He helped Clara inside, then closed the door behind her before returning to his seat. Clara felt the carriage lurch forward and settled into her seat, her head falling back. She closed her eyes, trying not to think of anything for at least a moment.

****

Clara took a week where she didn't do much of anything. Looking through some of her grandmother's things, she realized that of course she was going to have to decide what to do with her effects, but she couldn't bring herself to address that just yet.

In fact, about the only thing Clara could address was the small matter of bills. The small apartment she had shared with her grandmother at the Windermere wasn't luxurious, but it was a decent sized place, suitable for two women without men in their lives. Now, it seemed incredibly large for just one person, but it didn't change the fact that it was hers and that she was responsible for the monthly rent to be paid; rent that she was going to quickly find difficult to afford.

Clara was lucky in the sense that she had control over her grandmother's estate, as she was the last living relative, but the money there was dwindling quickly; since she had spent so much of the last three years not working, she didn't have much saved. She could make it a couple of months still, but soon a job would be necessary.

It was a daunting task to try to find a place to work, but Clara tried to be upbeat and hopeful about it. This was the start of her new life, she told herself.

On Monday morning, Clara grabbed a morning newspaper and began looking through the want ads. Her experience was limited, but she was a good, hard worker and was an excellent secretary. She was hopeful that she might find a suitable job.

Pencil in hand, Clara went through the ads, circling those that looked promising. There were several typist jobs and at least two clerical jobs that Clara felt she might be qualified for. As she was browsing the newspaper, Clara ran across a want ad.

MATRIMONIAL, it read. Established frontier man in search of a respectable young lady. Must be willing to travel a long distance in order to settle in a new area. Only those of agreeable character and good virtues need apply.

The address was included and Clara noted that it was in Montana. Frowning, Clara passed the paper to the side and smiled ruefully at herself.

"What are you thinking, Clara?" she asked the empty room.

Her mind needed to be focused on the here and now—and on paying the bills. But the ad stayed in her mind, even as she prepared to inquire about the jobs she had circled. If she was being honest with herself, it was the prospect of fulfilling a craving within her that kept her mind drifting back to that simple little request: a craving for connection and love.

Living alone did not seem like a terribly welcoming future.

Clara went to the businesses over on 61st, eager to find work, but discovered that she was to be turned down repeatedly.

"I have some experience," she told the man sitting at the desk.

He shuffled some papers before sighing. "I appreciate that, Ma'am, however, you're just not what we're looking for."

She'd heard that answer five times that day already and it caused her shoulders to slump to hear it again. "Thank you for your time, Sir," she told him politely. Taking up her crutches, she hobbled out, trying to ignore the stares she received as she did so.

By the time Clara returned home that day, she'd all but given up. She felt hopeless, certain that no one would take her. Maybe that was why she sat down with the dim light at her writing desk after combing her long blonde tresses. She had paper and her steel nib sitting in front of her; off to the side was the newspaper with the ad staring back at her.

It didn't have a name, so when she began the letter it sounded very informal:

To Whom It May Concern,

I am writing in regards to your matrimonial request. I must admit that I have never responded to such an ad before and am uncertain of the etiquette involved in it. There was no name listed in your ad, so I must also apologize for the formality of my letter.

I do hope you can forgive me.

Currently, my residence is in the City of New York, however, I have begun to think of changes adjusting my life. Montana seems a very long way away, but I do not fear travel. I'm afraid I have but a modest amount of savings and would not be able to contribute much, but as a frontier man, I suspect that you do not need my assistance in that area.

If you feel that perhaps we could be matched, I encourage you to respond.

Clara hesitated. The letter was terribly informal and didn't offer much in the way of personality from Clara, but then she was responding to an ad in the paper. It left her uncertain as to how she should sign it—and if she should include the most obvious thing about her: her braces.

Biting her lip, Clara decided to sign it Sincerely and added nothing more to the letter. Double checking the address, she sealed the note in an envelope and sent it off the following day before continuing her job hunting.

****

Clara received a response nearly three weeks after mailing off her hasty and impulsive letter to the mystery man in Montana. At first, she had been eager to hear back from him; nervous but excited. Now, as she checked for a return letter day after day, her eagerness had died down. She no longer expected any reply, much less one that might be positive.

That was why it surprised her so much to receive a personal letter from a Montana address.

Sitting at her desk, she stared at it for a long while. Did she care to open it? Did she dare to? In the weeks since she'd sent the letter things were... getting better. The place was still too big and her heart still ached over her loneliness, but she'd found solace in a new job. It didn't pay very well, and she was fairly certain that she'd received it from pity more than anything else, but she wasn't in a position to protest just then.

Before her mind had decided one way or the other, Clara's hand tore open the envelope and opened the letter. It was short, but spoke volumes to Clara.

Dear Clara,

I would take care of you to the utmost of my abilities. You would want for nothing here. I ask only one thing of you: be the cure for the aching loneliness in my heart.

Truest,

William Dean.

For several long moments, Clara's big hazel eyes stared down at the short, three sentence response she had received. So earnest were his words; so raw and filled with yearning. They touched something in Clara that had not been awoken during all her time on this Earth. With a shaking hand, she picked up her steel nib and began to write.

Mr. Dean,

I find that perhaps we share the same ache. Loneliness haunts my poor heart as well, and as I find myself alone in a city with so many, I wonder if your wild Montana might hold my cure.

Perhaps I am too foolish a girl to believe that a man so far from home might sway my life, but I believe that everything must happen for a reason. I could not speculate on Divine reason nor could I easily guess as to fate, but my life is in upheaval. I must believe that such change does not fall into one's life without a lining of silver.

I hope that you might be my silver lining and perhaps I might be yours.

Affectionately,

Miss Clara Burnell.

She sealed it in an envelope, carefully writing out the mailing address to be sure it was correct and slipped it into her bag. The bag went with her whenever she left home, making it easier to carry things with her cumbersome crutches. The thought made her question once again whether or not she should mention her disability.

"The letter is written already, Clara," she chided herself aloud. "Do not hinder yourself before you even have a chance."

****

Livingston, Montana, 1890

Clara had been on the train for nearly a week at this point, nearly three times as fast as any wagon would have taken her. It was a marvel that trains even went as far as Montana, but the locomotives seemed to be the greatest invention for the westward expansion to date. Clara was merely grateful that she might soon meet the man she could only hope would change her life.

When the passenger car finally came to a slow, chugging stop, Clara peeked out the window. As the steam cleared away from the train, she got a glimpse of the station; it looked mostly like the station in New York, though far simpler. There was a platform and an office, along with some benches, but otherwise she could see nothing but trees. It seemed as though the immediate area around the station was still heavily wooded, unlike her beloved New York.

The wheels screeched, steel against steel, and the caller began to announce that they'd arrived at their destination. "Livingston, Montana!" the man announced as Clara peeked her head out of the passenger room she shared with only one other, an older woman.

"Not too late to reconsider," the old woman informed Clara as she gathered up her bags. "Delicate thing like you ain't got no business in a difficult place like this."

Although harsh, the woman meant the words kindly and Clara felt bound to thank her for her concern. "Don't worry for me, ma'am," Clara told her with a brave smile. "I'm meeting someone here."

The woman eyed her for a moment. "A man? Is that man gonna take care of you?"

Hesitating only for a fraction of a second, Clara did her

best to stand up straighter with her crutches. "Yes. He is."

Letting out a sigh, the woman shook her head, muttering under her breath. All Clara caught of it was something about "better care at home." The woman left the room, then disappeared out into the hall.

Clara struggled to get her bag which held every one of William's letters as well as her papers and what little cash she'd scraped together. There was a trunk of hers in the luggage car as well, but they would collect those together later. Moving out into the hall, she found that there were several people moving towards the exits, but nothing like the number of passengers there had been when she got on. Trains had become one of the quickest ways to travel, and as a result, they were growing in popularity, but most people got off long before the likes of Montana. The people she did see were prospectors, mostly: men and a few less than reputable women who were taking advantage of the Homestead Act.

Clara allowed for most of these adventurous homesteaders to go ahead of her so that she could move at her own pace afterwards. She moved to the exit and then was kindly helped down by the caller who had announced their arrival.

"Now you be careful, young miss," he told her sincerely as she made it down to the platform.

Clara smiled at him gratefully, "Thank you for your kindness."

Clinging to both her bag and her crutches, Clara searched the platform for her future husband. They hadn't spoken much of physical appearance in their letters, though they had corresponded for nearly three months. At the time, it hadn't seemed all that important. Who cared what this man across the country looked like? She believed in her heart that if their souls matched, then the rest would fall into place. Maybe it was her own wishful thinking that he could see past her own disability, but she believed just the same.

There were several people standing alone; some of them holding signs, while others merely waved people over. Clara's heart hammered in her chest as she suddenly thought the worst: what if her dear William wasn't there?

Pushing the awful thought away, Clara went to the baggage man and pointed to her trunk. He hefted it onto the platform for her, then returned to the other passengers to do the same for them.

Standing beside her luggage, she realized how bad off she could be if William decided he was no longer interested in his bride from New York. Chewing on her lower lip, Clara once again scanned the crowd, hoping for some sign that indicated William was there waiting for her. As more and more people left the station, having found what they were looking for, Clara's hope withered. She didn't see anyone waiting for her; he wasn't coming.

Just as despair began to set in, Clara noticed a young man—handsome if a little roguish—searching the station. He wore a wide brimmed hat, like the cowboys down further south, and a thick coat that went almost to his knees. His hair was brown, dusting his shoulders, and his eyes were sharp and as blue as the Montana sky.

Clara's heart jumped in her chest. Could that be him?

Taking a risk, she moved as hurriedly as her crutches would allow; she didn't want him to leave. When she was close enough to call out, she nearly did, but her voice seemed caught in her throat. Worries swirled through her mind, the biggest of them centered on his reaction to her poor legs.

She was nearly three feet from him when his blue eyes finally settled firmly on her. His brow furrowed; his lips pulled into a frown. After a moment, a deep voice escaped his lips, "Miss Burnell?"

"Mr. Dean?" she asked breathlessly.

His eyes darted down to her crutches, his frown deepening, and for a moment she seemed certain that he would reject her. But then he offered to take her shoulder bag and asked, "Do you have other luggage, too?"

Clara nodded. "Yes. They've collected it from the train already; it sits on the platform."

He gave her a quick, curt nod, then moved toward her belongings. After he'd spoken to a man, he returned to Clara. "He'll load the trunk for us, then we must be on our way. I want to return home before we lose the light."

Home. This strange new land was Clara's home and this man beside her... well, he was to be her husband. The change was huge, but Clara welcomed it. She only hoped that William still felt the same.

****

The ride was by carriage, slow and arduous. Clara had already been traveling for quite some time and she was loathe to admit it, but she fell asleep almost immediately after entering the carriage. When she awoke, she was startled to realize that her head was resting lightly against William's strong shoulder.

Straightening up immediately, she looked away from his bright eyes. A blush graced her cheeks as she mumbled a feeble, "I'm sorry."

"Don't be. You've had a long trip." His voice was rough and he didn't look at her as he spoke.

William got out first, offering his hand to Clara once he was firmly on the ground. She gathered her crutches in one hand, and accepted his offered hand in the other. Unsteadily, she made it out of the carriage only to find that there was most definitely snow on the ground.

"Oh, I hadn't realized it had snowed so recently."

It was powdery and white, topping the massive trees all around them. As she surveyed the snow, she realized her surroundings had shifted dramatically. There was no sign of a road; the only building was a log cabin and the porch attached to it. Trees had overtaken the land almost completely, leaving them amidst a full grown forest. It was beautiful, if a little frightening. They seemed so far from everything.

William unloaded her trunk and then spoke for a moment with the man who drove the carriage. Dragging her trunk, William told her, "Follow me, dear. I'll show you where your room will be and I'll let my housekeeper, Mrs. Jones, know you're here."

Clara followed William into the relatively large cabin. It was certainly bigger than her apartment in New York, though by no stretch was it a mansion. There were two stories, a set of stairs leading to the second floor adjacent to the front door. Past the stairs was a hallway which led to at least two other rooms, one of which she presumed was Mrs. Jones' kitchen. The place was lovely, if a little rough; it very clearly lacked a woman's touch, indicated by the plain furniture and the lack of decoration. In fact, the only thing that Clara could find that seemed purely decorative was a bundle of white wildflowers sitting on the table just beside the door.

"These are lovely, Mr. Dean," she commented, wanting to fill up the silence.

"Please, call me William."

William had just begun to tug her truck up the stairs when she spoke. Looking up, his eyes followed her delicate hand to where it pointed at the flowers. He let out a sigh and shook his head, muttering something to himself that Clara couldn't catch. Immediately, she felt foolish for having said anything, worried that she'd said absolutely the wrong thing.

"I forgot them," William said, louder for her to hear this time. "I was supposed to bring them with me and I left them there on the table so I wouldn't forget. I did anyway."

Clara blinked. "What?"

"They're for you."

A warmth spread through Clara's chest even though they both fell silent afterwards. She slowly made her way up the stairs, a smile playing on her lips.

The stairs were difficult, but not impossible for Clara. It wasn't the first time she'd had to deal with them and crutches or no, she wouldn't let it detour her. William, however, was standing at the top of the stairs with a heavy frown on his lips.

"Perhaps Mrs. Jones should fix up a room downstairs

for you," he said suddenly when she was only halfway up the stairs. "It'll take a bit to get ready, but she can get a bed set up down there for you tonight."

Breathing moderately, Clara did her best to straighten up. She looked him right in the eye and informed him, "I am perfectly capable of managing stairs, thank you."

"Clara—"

It was the second time he'd said her name and it elicited the exact same reaction from her. A rush of warmth; a quickening of the beat of her heart.

William broke off, falling silent, and waited at the top of the stairs for her. When she reached the top, he escorted her down the hall to one of three doors. He pushed open the door, allowing her to go first.

"This will be your room, Miss Clara," he informed her.

It was a big enough room for just her and more than she was used to. There was a bed with plain white linens and a quilted bedspread that was embroidered with light purple flowers. Off to the side was a vanity with a mirror set into a wooden carving attached to the small desk. A chair accompanied it; both were painted white. Curtains hung across a small window towards the back and there was an armoire on the opposite side. The whole room was lovelier than Clara could have expected.

"I hope it's to your liking," William said uncertainly. "It was difficult to decide what might be most appropriate for you, so I had Mrs. Jones pick out some things. I wanted there to be something here for you when you arrived."

Clara felt her heart swell; he'd put so much thought and care into setting up her room. Turning to face him, she smiled sweetly. "I could not have wanted for anything better."

He offered her his first smile, small and tentative. Giving a small bow of his head, he said, "I'll leave you to get settled as I'm sure you're tired. There is a washroom at the end of the hall and my room, should you need me, is across from yours. If you're hungry, Mrs. Jones can have something set for you in an hour."

He turned to leave, but Clara stopped him.

"Isn't that part of my responsibilities?"

He hesitated, something clearly stopping him from speaking what was on his mind. "Later. For now, please get some rest."

With that, he left and closed the door after him. Clara stared at the door where he'd stood, wondering if he was having second thoughts. This room was beautiful and he was mindfully hospitable, but these things were also considered for an able young woman, not Clara. Pushing her uncertainties aside, Clara sat on the vanity seat, grateful for a break from her crutches. Staring in the mirror, she hoped that she could be what William was looking for; she'd already decided he was everything she had been in search of.

****

Clara had cleaned up as best she could and made her way down the stairs towards the kitchen. There were only a couple of doors in the hall and the first one ended up leading to the kitchen. When she walked in, Mrs. Jones was just finishing setting the table. The dishes weren't overly fancy, nor was the meal itself, but like everything else in the house, both were more than adequate.

William pulled out a chair for Clara, inviting her to sit.

"Thank you for all of this, William."

"Of course."

He sat opposite her on the other side of the table. During the meal, they ate in silence amidst flickering candlelight. Their meal of roasted pork and herbed potatoes was delicious, and Clara was inclined to tell him so.

"Mrs. Jones is a very talented cook."

"She's been fixing my meals for a while now," he admitted, glancing across the table at Clara.

"Well, hopefully her skills won't be necessary for much longer."

William fell silent, his brow furrowing as his mouth pulled down in a frown. His eyes looked away from Clara and he finished his meal without saying another word to her. Clara's hopes fell; this wasn't going to work.

When they'd both finished, Clara reached for her crutches and scooted herself back from the table. She got up, then bracing herself heavily on one side, she managed to take up her own plate. Immediately, William bolted up out of his seat.

"Now, Miss Clara, leave that for Mrs. Jones."

"Don't be ridiculous," she told him, trying to sound confident. "She cooked. The least I could do is take care of the mess."

William moved around the table quickly towards her, evidently not interested in allowing her to clean up. She was determined, however, to prove that she was useful and headed to the sink. Before she ever reached it, the plate tumbled from her grasp. It crashed to the floor, broken in three places. The room was swallowed up with silence, and Clara waited to be admonished.

The chastising never came, however. Instead, William came around the rest of the way and knelt down to clean up the pieces of the plate. Clara felt tears prick at her eyes as she warred between apologizing profusely and just leaving now so that he didn't have to deal with her and her clumsiness. Ultimately, as the tears began to spill down her full cheeks, Clara settled on a quiet "I'm sorry" and turned to leave the room. She went upstairs as quickly as her crutches would allow, then closed the door tightly when she'd reached her room.

What a mess I am, she thought miserably.

****

Tender morning light awoke Clara early the next morning. She had slept fitfully at best, worried that her clumsiness and her obvious physical disability were going to cost her a kind, gentle man. Dragging herself out of bed, Clara pulled her knitted shawl over her shoulders and sat at the vanity. She took only a few minutes to brush out her hair and pinned it up in a soft bun as swirling tendrils fell across her cheeks. Taking up her crutches, she went to the door. Cautiously, she peeked out into the hall; no one was there. With a steadying breath, Clara made her way out into the hall and down towards the washroom; she wanted to clean up that morning before going down to help Mrs. Jones with breakfast. After the fiasco that happened last night, she was determined to prove her worth to William.

As she passed William's door, it opened suddenly to reveal his rugged face and piercing blue eyes.

"Clara," he said, surprised. "I didn't realize you were awake."

Embarrassed, Clara looked away and pulled her shawl closer about her shoulders. "I only awoke moments ago, I'm afraid. I'll have to get used to country time."

He only nodded.

It seemed like he wasn't going to say anything more, so Clara continued towards the wash room. Just before she reached it, William called to her.

"I have some business to attend to in town. I'll be gone for a while, but please make yourself comfortable."

She looked back over her shoulder at him, disappointed by his words. Already he was finding excuses to be away from her and she found that she couldn't hold it against him. She offered a faint smile and nodded.

"Clara—" he broke off, seeming to think something

over. Finally, he said, "I hate to leave you, but Mrs. Jones can keep you company. I've started a fire downstairs and there's a comfortable seating area there. Stay warm until I come back."

With that, he left, heading immediately downstairs. Clara remained frozen listening to his footsteps as they grew fainter and fainter. Finally, she heard the door close. A sigh escaped her lips as she made her way to the washroom to clean up.

****

It was late, darkness already beginning to fall, when William arrived home that day. He came in through the front door, kicking his boots against the wall to knock off the mud and snow that had collected there.

Clara heard him from the kitchen and felt her heart thump excitedly in her chest. She had come up with a plan today to convince him that she wasn't a lapse in his judgement: she had insisted on preparing the meal for this evening herself, leaving Mrs. Jones free to run errands for the day. The food was nearly ready, and Clara moved about the kitchen to set the table, taking her time so that she didn't drop anything. She wanted everything to be set when he came in to find her, and maybe then he would believe that she was useful.

"Clara?" he called from the living room. She heard a heavy thump and what sounded like wood tumbling together. "I brought more firewood. Wasn't sure if there was enough already here for you..."

He trailed off and she heard his boots clopping on the floor as he came closer.

"Clara?"

He turned the corner into the kitchen just as Clara finished setting the table. Immediately, he froze. His eyes surveyed the kitchen, then arrived to her. His bright blue gaze pierced through her; she could hardly seem to breathe.

"What is all this?" he demanded, his voice low.

Clara felt her heart wilt, all her excitement deflating. He didn't like it, not one little bit.

"It's... it's dinner. I wanted it to be ready when you got home."

He said something quickly under his breath. She didn't catch it, but she thought it might have been a swear word.

Taking his wide brimmed hat off, he placed it on the counter off to the side.

Shaking his head, he said, "I wish you wouldn't do that, Miss Clara. Mrs. Jones should be doing the cooking; you don't need to be tiring yourself out like that."

A surge of anger swept Clara. How dare he insinuate that she was incapable of the simplest tasks? Her mouth had about run away with itself when she paused. She saw the concern crinkling at the edges of his eyes; his mouth was set in a line of worry. And just like that, her anger disappeared. She couldn't be angry with him for worrying over her. Wasn't that the first step towards love?

She hoped so.

"Well, it is already made," she told him, taking a seat before he could move around the table to pull out the chair for him, "and the table is already set. I wish you might sit with me and enjoy it so that it doesn't go to waste."

It took him a long moment, but he finally pulled out the chair opposite Clara and sat.

Dinner was much like it had been the previous night: quiet. The talking was non-existent until halfway through the meal and then, out of the blue, William broke the silence.

"I don't mean to pry, Miss Clara, and please tell me if I have overstepped some sort of social boundary, but I must ask: how was it that you came by those braces and crutches?"

Her crutches were leaning against the edge of the table within easy reach of her. They were polished wood, expensive and almost beautiful if one could forget their purpose, but Clara hardly thought he was asking about them specifically. No, he was asking about her accident and that was the most polite way he could think to bring up her disability.

"When I was just a girl, no older than sixteen, my grandmother took me to the stables there in New York," Clara began, folding her napkin two, then three times, though it hardly needed it. "She informed me that all young women of any good breeding had best learn the importance and elegance of riding. So I did."

A wistful smile crossed Clara's face as she thought back on the hopes and dreams of her younger self. Once, she had thought she might be the best at riding—even a professional. Though she had no long term desire to be one of those new 'working women,' she had thought that before marriage, she might teach as a riding instructor for young girls. But that was all a very long time ago now.

"One day, while riding, a terrible storm rolled in. All of the horses were being brought inside, but I was still out. I had ridden too far and it took time for me to return to the safety of the stables. Too much time, it would seem. Lightning tore through the sky, spooking my poor stallion. He threw me from his back and—"

Clara broke off, feeling tears begin to form in her eyes. She blinked rapidly, desperate to keep them from falling. The horse, in its panic, trampled her legs; how quickly fate had turned against her.

"The doctors did what they could," Clara continued, "but they promised me that I would never walk without these braces and crutches again."

The dining room fell silent and Clara could not bring herself to look up and see the expression on William's face. Would it be one of pity? Of disgust?

"I am sorry for your tragedy, Miss Clara," he told her. Then he pushed his chair back, scraping it along the floor as he stood. "Please leave the cleanup for Mrs. Jones."

He left before Clara could ever work up the courage to

look at him.

****

William returned late just as he had for the last six days in a row. Since Clara had arrived, he'd spent what seemed like only a handful of stolen moments with her. She'd done her best to become useful to Mrs. Jones and adapt to the loneliness of living so far from her neighbors. Although she hadn't had much of a social life in New York since she spent so much of her time taking care of her ailing grandmother, there had still been an influx of people surrounding her. Living in an apartment building, as the styles in that part of the country permitted, had offered her the chance to go out in search of company, even if she didn't have a large amount of truly close friends.

Here in Montana on William's expansive property, she found that she was more lonesome than ever before. People were miles away in town over difficult terrain that was potentially dangerous if the snow came down heavily. Worse still, the only way into town was by horse.

William had a carriage, it was true, but one of the wheels had come off and he had yet to find the chance to fix it. It left Clara in a bad spot, because even if she wanted to leave, there was no way for her to do so. She was incapable—and a little terrified of—riding alone.

When William came in the front door, Clara was downstairs curled up on the couch. She had taken to reading, finding that he had a fair number of interesting books along the walls of the room she had to guess was a study of some kind. The first few days William had been disappearing, Clara had attempted to help Mrs. Jones with the cooking and cleaning, but after the fiasco that seemed to happen every time—William would come home and tell her that she shouldn't have done that, and that Mrs. Jones would take care of those tasks—she finally gave in. There was just no point in making dinner or tidying the house if it only made him unhappy.

So she began to read. Stories filled her head for the hours that William was gone; they were the only things that took away the fear of rejection that seemed to build every day.

Tonight, he came in through the front door as he always did, kicked his boots against the wall and took off his hat. His bright blue eyes found Clara sitting in front of the fire reading one of his books once again. That was one of the things about him that Clara admired; he always seemed to approve of her reading.

"Miss Clara," he greeted. His voice had begun to take on a softness to it, growing it seemed with each day that she was there. "Have you enjoyed your reading today?"

Clara did her best to finish her sentence without letting him distract her and marked her place in the book. Putting it to the side, she finally looked up at him. "Yes, it's quite fascinating to read about the first settlements."

"I'm glad you think so."

For a moment, William stood there staring at her. This was where their conversations often broke off, William uncertain where to take them and Clara worried that she might disappoint him once more. So he turned away, prepared to head towards the kitchen to ask Mrs. Jones what she had prepared for supper. Before he could reach the kitchen, however, Clara stopped him with her voice as she called out.

"William? Where do you go every day?"

She had been terrified to ask this question, worried that she already knew the answer. Where else would a gentleman, no longer able to spend his free time alone at home, be doing all day in town? He was avoiding her, and was quite possibly spending time with other women. She didn't believe so, trusting in the candor of his letters, but it was hard to dispel her own treacherous worries.

"Into town. You know that."

Gathering up her crutches, Clara rose to her feet, turning to face him. "But what do you do in town all day? What is so important there that you must spend all day every day away from your—"

Clara stopped midsentence. She couldn't call herself his wife, though she hoped that it would eventually come to pass.

William turned to look at her, an unreadable expression on his face. After a long moment of silence, he said, "Why don't you come with me and find out?"

Eyes widening in surprise, Clara's heart suddenly bursting with hope, she found that she couldn't answer him right away. She didn't know what to say to this sudden offer.

He continued on, his words hurried, "I would of course have to fix the carriage first. I wouldn't ask you to ride horseback with me; that would be entirely inappropriate."

"I... that would... I would love to go," Clara finally managed to get out, smiling widely.

"Give me two days to fix the carriage."

They had dinner not long after that; neither of them said much. It was the same as any other night she'd spent there with him, except that for once, there was hope brimming inside her.

****

For two days, Clara watched William work on the carriage. He still continued to spend most of his day in town, but every day when he came home, he would work a little to fix the wheel on the carriage. It was clear that he was tired, exhausted even, but he kept his word to Clara; two days later, the carriage was ready.

Clara was up bright and early that morning, but still not before William. He was already dressed and ready to go, waiting for her at the base of the stairs while she made her way slowly down them. When she reached the bottom, he held the door for her and followed her out. He opened the door of the carriage for Clara, but she hesitated before climbing inside.

It was clear that he had no driver and the horses most definitely couldn't be allowed to drive themselves. William would have to act as driver, sitting outside while she sat alone inside.

Turning to William, she made a request. "Would you be so kind as to grab an extra quilt from the living room? I worry it might be cold along the way."

William was quick to do as she asked, hurrying back inside. While he was busy retrieving her quilt, Clara moved as quickly as she could. Using an old crate as a stepping stool, Clara placed one of her crutches off to the side and with her free hand managed to step up and pull herself up into the driver's bench. She placed both of her crutches along the bottom to keep them within easy reach, but out of the way, and then waited. When she heard William return, she straightened her back and squared her shoulders, determined to not allow him to talk her down.

"Clara, what are you—?" William began, but Clara interrupted him.

"We had best hurry. I don't want to be out after dark."

William looked as though he wanted to argue with her, but after letting out a sigh, he closed the door to the carriage and climbed up next to her. He spread the quilt around her, tucking it in as best he could to keep her warm.

"Next time, I would rather you sat in the carriage," he told her, as he urged the horses forward.

"Well, I would prefer to sit with you."

William said nothing in response.

It was a long ride into town and not easy. They went slow, so that the carriage wouldn't bust along the way and Clara wouldn't be jostled about too much, but even then, the roads were muddy and uninviting. Eventually, however, they did arrive in the town of Livingston.

William pulled the carriage to a stop outside of a respectable looking building with a sign hanging over the door: Dr. James Albers.

"A doctor's office?" Clara asked in alarm, suddenly worried that William's frequent trips into town were concerned with his health.

William had already climbed down and had produced a stepping stool to help her down. She handed her crutches to him first, which he set along the side of the carriage, then gingerly began to climb down. She knew that her legs wouldn't carry any weight, so she tried to use the strength of her arms. It wasn't enough, however, and she nearly fell—right into the arms of William. He grabbed her about the middle, pulling her close so that she wouldn't fall.

For one lingering moment, Clara felt his warmth engulf her, filling her with emotion. Their eyes met and Clara realized that there was nowhere else she would rather be, no matter how far she lived from other people, no matter how difficult it might be to live out in the wilderness as she did.

The moment was broken as William realized how close they were. He eased her down gently until she was seated on the stepping stool, then released her. Reaching for her crutches, he gave them to her one at a time and then helped her to a standing position.

"Is this your lady, William?"

Clara looked up, startled by the new voice. An older man with graying hair and a full, but trim beard stood behind William. He wore a pair of round spectacles over which he looked down at the pair of them. There was a smile on his face.

"Dr. Albers," William greeted. Making sure first that Clara was stable, he went to the older man and shook hands. "Yes, this is her. Dr. Albers, I would be delighted to introduce you to my... future wife, Miss Clara."

****

Clara was quickly learning that the day would be full of surprises, the first of which had been the revelation that William still had every intention of marrying Clara. The second she uncovered as she sat in the office of Dr. Albers.

"I am a surgeon, Miss Clara," Dr. Albers explained in a calm, gentle voice. "I've been friends with young William here ever since he was a boy. It was indeed a coincidence to find that we had both arrived in Montana, but I am happy to have rediscovered our friendship."

Glancing between Dr. Albers and William, Clara found herself confused. Her head swam with questions; what did this have to do with her?

William reached out for Clara's hand, surprising her as he encased her small fingers in his large calloused ones. Heat rushed through her, a blush gracing her cheeks.

"William has been stopping by every day to discuss options," Dr. Albers continued. "I'll admit, I was a bit skeptical at first when he described your condition, but after some discussion of the cause and talk of the procedure, I think there is hope. Seeing you has convinced me that if anyone deserves this second chance, it is you, my dear."

Procedure. Blood surged through Clara's veins as her heart thundered beneath her breast. Could he possibly be suggesting what she thought he was?

"Clara, I would like to repair your legs."

Clasping her hand between both of his, William knelt down beside her chair, his expression open and earnest as he looked into her eyes. "Since the first letter I'd ever received from you, I knew that I loved you, Clara. Maybe I was worried to admit it at first, but before you came here, I'd already decided that I was yours. Then you arrived on that train and I saw you."

Sadly, Clara whispered, "You saw my disability."

William shook his head. "No, I saw the most beautiful woman in the world, hurt by a cruel twist of fate. I begged Dr. Albers to help you. It took some convincing; he was really worried that there was no hope, but then I told him how strong you were. How determined. I knew that if there was anything I could do to help you, I had to do it. Please, Clara, I know that I am a man who is rough around the edges, but I think with your patience, I can be a better man. Will you still have me as your husband, my dearest Clara?"

Tears filling her eyes, she choked back a sob of joy. "Oh yes, William. Yes!"

In his excitement, William lifted her up in the chair, holding her tightly. It wasn't until Dr. Albers cleared his throat that William eased her back into her seat.

"Now, I think it's time to discuss your operation."

****

Three months ago, Clara would have said that there were some things in this world that were simply impossible, the least of which would be her ability to walk again without the use of leg braces and crutches. But life had its own plans and fate had brought her to the one man who could change her world forever.

Clothed in the most beautiful white dress Clara had ever owned, a floor length, high necked dress with lace trim and pearl buttons, she walked down the aisle towards the only man she had ever loved. William stood, his face open and inviting, at the other end of the church. He looked dashing in a formal suit, waiting for his bride.

With a wide smile gracing her lips, Clara walked with her own legs, unassisted towards the man who had changed her life. When the reverend asked her if she would take William as hers forever, she answered without hesitation: "Yes."

They settled on William's plot of Montana land as man and wife. Clara turned his house into a home; William provided her the safety and security she had always dreamed of. When Clara became pregnant the first time, she thought it was a miracle that would never come to pass, but in June she gave birth to a baby boy they named James—after the doctor who had given Clara back the use of her legs and changed her entire life forever.

THE END

Montana Mail Order Bride Emma

Hartford, Connecticut - 1875

"To Mrs. Emma Hammersley," read little Margaret, who was still so small despite being nearly twelve years old. "We regret to inform you that we shall not be able to financially support your family any longer. Although we sympathize with your unfortunate situation, we do not feel that it is our responsibility to continue to support a family that no longer includes our deceased son. Best, The Hammersley Estate."

When Margaret put down the letter, she glanced up at her mother with huge eyes. They were the bright blue color of her father's and looked odd being so large in such an otherwise small body. Many had asked if poor Margaret was sickly and commented how it was bad enough that she was a girl; to be sick, too, was just an awful lot for a poor mother to bear. Emma had never placed much stock in their opinions, however, and staunchly believed that her beautiful little girl was simply a late bloomer.

"Mother, does this mean we have been disowned?"

Emma pursed her lips together tightly; what was she supposed to tell her sweet child? Spooning up the porridge into a small bowl, she placed it on the table in front of her daughter, suddenly regretting that she had insisted that Margaret read the letter at all. It was their tradition; the very early morning was a time for reading and the further expansion of young Margaret's mind. Most days it was the previous day's paper that Emma had her daughter read, however, when she had seen that Mrs. Hammersley had sent a letter, she thought it was the perfect opportunity to read something of a more personal note. She should have known that the devilish old woman had never taken a liking to her or her young daughter, and would write nothing but spiteful things in correspondence.

"It means that we are finally free of your mean-spirited grandmother," Emma told her with a wrinkle of her nose and a quick wink of her hazel eyes.

Margaret grinned at her mother as she took up her spoon. When Emma brought her own bowl to the table and sat down across from her daughter, they both began to eat. It was a quiet meal, Emma's thoughts too troubled by her mother-in-law's unkind letter. She wasn't quite sure what to do, realizing that things were slowly getting harder and harder for her tiny family.

Oh, if only poor James had survived, Emma thought sadly to herself.

When the sun started peeking through the window, Margaret glanced up in surprise—and dread. It was time for the both of them to go. Emma gathered up the dishes and placed them in the washtub for later, then they both grabbed their coats before heading out the door. They had to go down nearly five flights of stairs thanks to the new multistory building they'd had to move into last year. Holding tightly to Margaret's hand, Emma headed out the front door towards the street. They weren't far from the factory, thankfully, so they walked instead of trying to hail a hack carriage; they couldn't afford it anyway.

As they hurried towards the Brown building, Emma noticed young Mr. Mannford who always sold newspapers on the street. She paused to buy one, paid and thanked him, then went on her way.

"I know it's a long day, my darling, but we must do this."

Emma smoothed out the sweet curls that hung about her daughter's pale face. Smiling, she knelt down and kissed her on the cheek; they would have to part here.

"I know, mother," Margaret said in a small voice. She had only been going to the factory for a few weeks, though the toll it was taking on her was quickly becoming evident. Emma would give everything she had in the world to have the money to once more send her little girl to gain the formal education those of a higher class might receive. Had James still been alive—or if James's mother weren't so dead set against including them in the family—it would have been possible.

"It's only for a little longer," Emma promised. "Soon, fortune will smile on us again and we will be whisked away from this life."

"Yes, mother."

"I promise you, things will get better, my little darling."

With that, Emma watched as her only child scampered up the steps into the factory building where she would work for the next ten hours. She wasn't the only girl to head up those steps—their ages ranging between six and fourteen—but Emma couldn't help but think that she was the most precious.

When Margaret disappeared inside the doors—she would have to travel up three flights to find the room where she would spend her day sewing waistcoats— Emma turned away and headed down to her own job. She, too, was a seamstress, making on average only a little more than her young daughter. Neither of their wages would be enough to hold them for much longer, but it was all she could do for now.

Gripping the paper tightly in her hand, she hoped that perhaps it held the answers she was so desperately searching for.

****

When Emma arrived home that evening, Margaret was already sitting in the modest living room, entranced as she listened to an all too familiar voice. Emma smiled wearily and hung up her coat before joining the two as they read their stories.

"...and she fell away into the water, nothing but foam and wishes."

The man sitting in the rocking chair closed the book, one of Margaret's favorites about a siren and a lost maiden, and glanced up at Emma. With a bright smile, he rose from the chair and headed over to her. "Emma!"

Returning his smile, Emma allowed herself to embrace her longtime friend. "Frederick! When did you return from your trip? I thought surely you would be another month."

"Nonsense. With our modern railroad advances, the potential of which does not stop, it marvels me only that it has taken so long."

Grinning, Margaret scrambled to her feet and rushed over to wrap her arms tightly about her mother's middle. Since she was still working in the child factory, her hours could be no longer than ten a day by law. Emma's, of course, were quite extended from that, and she was exhausted. But she was happy to see her daughter and was delighted to have found that Frederick returned.

"Have you eaten?" Emma questioned her daughter.

She nodded vigorously. "Oh yes. Frederick cooked a lovely meal, with pheasant and everything!"

"That's wonderful." Turning to Frederick, she asked, "How was your trip? Will you stay for long this time?"

"Oh, I would like to. Very much so." He smiled fondly at Emma, then, they moved to the sitting room once again.

The next two hours consisted of tales from Frederick's journeys—many of which they'd already heard, though some were more recent—and Margaret begging to be allowed to stay up later still. Eventually, she fell asleep all on her own and Frederick carried her to bed. When she was tucked in, the two adults returned to the sitting room—Emma had important business to discuss.

Pouring them each a cup of tea, Emma retrieved her newspaper from earlier that morning. Unfolding it, she found the page she was looking for: it was the section of the newspaper featuring advertisements of all kinds. Originally, Emma had been searching it with the hopes of finding a job that might result in better pay—and the possibility that her daughter might again attend formal education.

"Emma, dearest," Frederick began, concern clouding his normally handsome features. "What has you so worried? Is it little Margaret? I do wish you would let me help you with your troubles."

Emma shook her head vehemently. "I have told you already, I will take no charity. My poor little family is not your responsibility and how might I feel if I took advantage of the kindness of my dear James's best and truest friend? No, I simply won't have it."

Frederick let out a sigh that indicated he might be inclined to argue with her about it again. They had gone round and round with it dozens of times before, ever since James's untimely death. His offer was surely genuine and his heart was filled with nothing but the best of intentions, but Emma could not force herself to take from someone she was so fond of. The responsibility of her state was either that of her family—which was clearly not the Hammersleys—or that of her husband. As Frederick was neither, she could not accept his generous offer.

Before Frederick could begin the age-old argument, Emma quickly brought his attention to the newspaper. "I am concerned, I will admit," she began, searching for the right ad. "It pains me to see poor Margaret denied the opportunities of other young girls her age simply because of my unfortunate state and her grandmother's vindictiveness."

"That old bat has never liked you," Frederick told her angrily. "All she has ever cared for was money and high society. Ridiculous."

Emma smiled kindly at Frederick, grateful for his support. Old Mrs. Hammersley had never been unkind to Frederick, who came from a wealthy family just a little farther south, but she had always despised Emma. Once, she had even called her the downfall of the family's good name. In all reality, it should have come as no surprise that Emma and her daughter would be cut from the Hammersley's ties.

"I'm afraid her disdain for us has reached an unfortunate peak," Emma admitted, still searching the paper. "I received a letter today and I imagine it is the final one."

"What did she say now?"

"She has told me that she cannot support us and that she asks that I no longer write her."

Although Emma had managed to be strong that morning in front of her daughter, sitting up so late at night with Frederick, she couldn't hold back the onslaught of feelings. How unfair it all seemed! Tears formed behind her eyes and she tilted her head back, blinking rapidly in an attempt to clear them before they fell. One small drop escaped from the corner of her eye and she was startled to feel the soft caress of a man's hand wipe it away.

She pulled her head up and stared over at Frederick. His expression was full of intensity, trying to express something that Emma couldn't understand, or perhaps

71

simply wasn't ready to. He opened his mouth, eyebrows pulled together in sympathy, ready to say something, but Emma wouldn't let him.

She couldn't. It was sympathy that was written across his features and she couldn't hear it pour from his mouth, too. So, she jumped forward; she pulled the paper to her, finally spotting the ad she had been searching for.

"I think I will respond to this ad." She pointed to it, showing it to Frederick.

He seemed to debate whether or not to press the subject of whatever he had been so intent on telling her before sighing and looking to her paper. She pointed out the small ad:

MATRIMONIAL—A successful American bachelor, forty-two years of age, seeks a respectable woman of a moderate age for immediate marriage. Must be family oriented and desirous of a large family. Preferred skills include cooking, cleaning, and timely management of daily activities. Those above the age of forty need not apply.

There was an address attached to the ad as well indicating that the bachelor lived out west in Livingston, Montana. It would be a long, arduous journey, despite the advancements of the railroad that Frederick had boasted of earlier in the evening. The West was a dangerous, wild place as many were apt to tell Emma. Full of outlaws and prospectors alike, most of that part of the country was still raw terrain waiting for civilized people to cultivate it. Emma didn't know how committed she might be to such an adventure, but she knew that she was committed to the success and well-being of her only child. A man who had found his success out west might be her only opportunity to give her daughter a real chance at a good life.

Placing the newspaper down on the table, a deep frown etched into his handsome features, Frederick didn't look at her as he asked, "Surely you are not actually considering the likes of this?"

"I am," she protested, attempting to sound firm, though in her heart she was terrified. "Our lives here have grown difficult to the point where I fear I will not be able to take care of my darling daughter much longer. James's family has demonstrated how little they care for me and my working is simply not enough to provide for my little girl."

Emma had been practicing her speech and her reasoning all day; she'd been hoping she would have been able to make arrangements before Frederick arrived. The danger of responding to such an ad did not escape her keen mind, however, she understood the necessity of it. Certain risks had to be taken; she only wished that she need not introduce her daughter to those same risks. All day, she had been trying to think of a way to keep her daughter safe even if her own safety could not be assured. In the end, she had come up with only one thing: Frederick.

Reaching out, Emma placed her hands atop his, their warmth seeping into her cold fingers. "We are desperate," Emma admitted in a small voice. "And I..." she hesitated, uncertain if she was ready to share something so deeply personal, even with Frederick. Finally, she told him, "I am not ready to spend the last of my days alone. I am a widow, but I am a woman, too."

Conflict raced across Frederick's features, his soft brown eyes filled to the brim with worry and affection for her. There seemed to be torment there, too—she presumed it was due to being in such a position as he was, yet unable to help her.

"And there is no one here... so much closer to your home that you might find to... to fill that void left by someone so dear to your heart?" Frederick's words were careful, tip-toeing around something that perhaps should have been obvious to Emma, yet still seemed to elude her.

Shaking her head, soft blonde curls slipped out of the pins meant to hold them up and drifted across her cheeks. "Who would I find here? I have no time for society parties to meet an eligible man, and those whom I might engage with on odd occasion have no interest in the likes of me. No, if I am to find a man, then I am afraid I shall have to look far beyond the walls of home."

Something eased in Frederick's expression, though it was not a sign of relief. Instead, it was a mark of resignation; he had accepted that she would not be swayed.

Finally, he said to her, "Very well, my dearest Emma. If you must respond to such an ad, then I must insist upon one thing only."

Frowning, Emma asked him hesitantly, "And what is that?"

"That I make the long trek to Montana with you. As your chaperone."

****

Harrisburg, Pennsylvania - 1875

Emma clung tightly to Margaret's hand as she tried to follow as closely to Frederick as the station would allow. At least half a dozen times, they'd gotten separated and he'd had to come and find them. It was difficult with so many people, and with a bag in one hand and a child in the other, it was no wonder at all she was having difficulty keeping up. To his credit, Frederick of course was carrying the majority of the luggage. Once they actually arrived at their train and were beginning to board, there would be room in the baggage car for their luggage, and officials who worked for the station would be all too happy to help them. Until then, he carried most of their things, leaving Emma with only one small bag to contend with and Margaret only her porcelain doll, a gift from her father years ago.

After a moment, Emma realized that she had once again lost sight of Frederick. He was a tall man with soft dark hair that was quite thick and very well maintained, and though she felt he was quite attractive, he blended in easily with the large crowd there at the Baltimore & Ohio station. Everyone seemed to be wearing the same dark coat as him, carrying the same amount of luggage, each with the same dark hair. The features she might find distinguishing were in his face, so open and soft, carrying with it a sweetness that never failed to make a smile ease across her lips.

Panic began to work its way into her chest; they only had a few minutes more before they needed to be on the train. "Frederick?" she tried calling, though amidst the tooting of steam and the blowing of whistles, she couldn't even hear herself as she called for him.

Trying to stay calm for Margaret's sake, Emma's hazel eyes searched the station in hopes of spotting him. She was about to call his name again when a hand gripped on her shoulder, making her jump and cry out, "Oh!"

"Emma, there you are!"

It was Frederick, looking just as frazzled as she felt, if that was possible. Relief crossed his features when he found the both of them.

"I'm so sorry!" Emma apologized immediately, as Frederick steered them towards a set of steps leading up towards the entrance to the train. "I tried to follow you, but this crowd is impossible! I never would have imagined—"

"It's alright, Emma," Frederick soothed easily. "I wouldn't leave you behind."

Warmth eased through Emma, a sense of security returned now that she was once again with Frederick. His kindness ensured that nothing terrible would happen to her and her daughter.

Frederick was familiar with traveling, because he dealt so often with both land prospectors and other realty agencies which required him to travel beyond his Hartford home. Margaret always told him he had such a boring job, but she never complained when he told her of his trips. It made for interesting stories of far off places to tell to them; he had no family of his own beyond his mother and father. In addition, it proved that, regardless of his family's independent and inherited wealth, Frederick was a hard worker, determined to make his own mark in the world. It was the new American way and happened to be a trait that Emma very much admired in her dear friend. Now, however, she was simply grateful that his experience with travel allowed her and Margaret's safe passage into the Wild West a little less daunting.

Pennsylvania was the nearest station to pick up the Baltimore & Ohio train headed west, as Frederick told them, which meant they'd had to take a carriage all the way to the station. She was just grateful they wouldn't have to go by wagon all the way to Montana! From what she understood, it was quite the journey. Later, in Minnesota, they would have to transfer companies altogether, but at least the same railway could take them most of the way there.

The three of them shuffled in behind a growing line of people attempting to get on board. It was difficult, Emma being jostled about because there was such a large crowd. Many were attempting to get on the train, but others were merely there to bid their loved ones good bye and to wish them safe travels. It made Emma feel a little claustrophobic; although her days at work were in a relatively small room with a multitude of other young women, in the end it was still nothing like this. It didn't help that she was already nervous about the things to come and she was unfamiliar with lengthy travel like this.

Emma had been away from Hartford only twice in her life; Margaret had been only once. The first trip away had been originally planned right after her formal engagement to James. Of course, things didn't quite go as planned. She had never met his family before and he insisted that, of course, she must at least once meet the elder Hammersleys. She agreed, hopeful that the family she was being brought into would be as warm and welcoming as she had always dreamed. Her own family had died of illness and misfortune, a curse that seemed to follow her into her adult life years later, leaving her with little beyond her determination to survive. When she'd met James, it had been a bit of a whirlwind romance; he was everything she could have hoped for. The prospect of his family—the older, motherly matron and the firm, but warm father—had been so inviting to her that she'd all but jumped for joy at the thought of meeting them. They were denizens of North Carolina, making their fortune before President Lincoln ever took office. Ultimately, the Civil War prevented their trip into the South—tensions were too high and it was simply deemed too dangerous to risk such a trip over a thing like engagement. When they finally did manage to meet James's family, it was already two years after they'd been married and the war was finally over. Margaret was a year and a half old, and when they all traveled down to North Carolina, tensions were still high and the Hammersleys were incredibly cold. They never went again.

The only other time Emma had been out of Hartford was for their honeymoon. It had been an exciting trip to the New York countryside. Shortly after that, Margaret had been born and they didn't travel again until the war was over.

Within seven years of Margaret's birth, James had taken ill and by the time the poor child was only eight, her father had perished.

Emma had become a widower at only twenty-seven years of age. At the time, she believed vehemently that she could never again love a man so much as she had loved her dear James. But time crept on without him; her grief subsided. Although she would never forget her lost love, she admitted to herself that her heart was strong enough to try again.

As they boarded the train, Frederick presented all of their tickets and the man at the door waved them inside. There were several different cars full of seating arrangements; Frederick led them to a relatively secluded area and stored their bags away. Margaret immediately dove for a window to glance outside at all the people who remained on the platform, waving and kissing at their counterparts on the train.

The three of them settled into their seats, and several moments later, the train left the station.

It was an odd sensation to feel the movement of the train; different from the feeling of a hackney cab. There was a chug-chug sound and motion that went with it that was equal parts soothing and strange. For a long while, Margaret asked questions about the train—and about Montana, where they were ultimately heading—and all but plastered her little face and wide eyes up against the glass to look out the window. When it finally grew dark, Margaret began to yawn and settled down. Eventually, she wound up with her head in Emma's lap.

Emma slowly combed her fingers through her daughter's silky curls; their car was mostly quiet with either sleep or thoughtfulness.

"She is exhausted, the poor little thing," Emma whispered quietly to Frederick so as not to wake her child.

Frederick was sitting across from the two of them, looking fondly on little Margaret, as affectionately as any father might. "It is a long trip for someone so young." He looked up at Emma, the tender expression on his face shifting to one of thoughtfulness. "And you? How are you feeling? It is a long trip for a young woman as well."

Emma gave a gentle shrug of her shoulders. "I am quite alright, I assure you. Not even tired, actually." She laughed a little, quiet and nervous. Smiling ruefully at her chaperone, she admitted, "I'm nervous. It's such a long distance to travel for a complete stranger."

Frederick's lips pursed tightly together, and for a long moment, he didn't say anything at all, the sound of the moving train the only noise filling the car. When he finally spoke, his voice was softer than she anticipated. "It is not too late to reconsider."

Emma's eyes widened in surprise. Stifling a sudden small laugh, she said, "Frederick, we are already on the train! We have bought our tickets, given my landlord notice and packed up everything I own! If anything, I think it is entirely too late, wouldn't you say?"

She said it lightly, almost teasing, but inside it was more of a panicked response. In all actuality, she was quite terrified of what was to come. What if the ad in the paper was merely a ruse and the man wasn't interested in a wife at all? She had heard of dozens of terrible scams by men out west, taking in poor naïve women who simply didn't know any better—or who were too desperate to not take the risk. She had shared only a half a dozen letters with the man—his name was Henry—and while he certainly seemed like an honorable, legitimate man, there was simply no way to know for certain if he was the man he claimed to be. Not until she arrived with her twelve-year-old daughter in tow.

Oh, the relief she had felt when Frederick insisted on being her chaperone. It was a terrible inconvenience to him, she knew, but she could not muster up the courage to say no to him. He was her last friendly face and she couldn't let him go.

"I would pay for your return," Frederick told her almost immediately, his eyes bright and his tone moderately insistent. It was almost as if he were eager for her to reconsider. "We can get off at the next station in Indiana and take the next immediate train back East to Hartford. It would likely take an additional day or two, but we would hardly be in a predicament. And as for living arrangements, I have a summer house that would be most suitable for—"

Emma placed one hand over her chest in an effort to stop the sudden rapid beating of her lonely heart and held the other one up to stop him from continuing his entirely too generous offer. She was surprised by his vehemence; he was always kind, but this seemed excessive. The laugh that had originally been just at the tip of her tongue, more hysterical than amused, died immediately. He was clearly worried about her.

Turning serious, Emma told him, "There is no longer anything left for me in Hartford, though I do love it so. My future is in Montana, as is Margaret's."

She glanced down at her daughter, sleeping peacefully despite the intensity of their discussion.

"Do you truly and honestly believe that you will find love with this... this stranger?"

There was a pleading note in Frederick's voice that made Emma look up at his face. It, too, was filled with an imploring expression, his eyes speaking volumes to her. She once again felt that this was all too much of a reaction from him. He had been James's closest friend, and certainly her favorite of the bunch. As James's friend, he felt obligated to look out for the family dear James left behind, but sometimes Emma felt that this loyalty would be his downfall. Certainly, he didn't owe them generosity of this degree.

He is such a good, loyal friend, she thought, and wondered if that loyalty wasn't clouding his judgment in this particular matter—or perhaps, like a good friend, he wanted only her happiness in the end.

Emma wished that she could simply lie and tell him that the few short correspondence letters from her matrimonial suitor had been enough to spark a fire of love within her. But she couldn't. It was a lie, and she couldn't bring herself to lie to such a dear a friend, so she was as honest as she could bring herself to be: "I cannot love a man I do not know. But I am endeavoring with letters and this very trip to learn who that man is. Love grows with time; perhaps, then, I can grow to love him."

It was what she hoped for, though one of her greatest fears was to find that there could never be love between them and she would spend the rest of her days loveless.

"Very well," Frederick told her stiffly, his expression almost one of pain. "I can hope for nothing but the best and will do my greatest effort as your chaperone to ensure your personal happiness. You have my word."

"Thank you, Frederick. Your kindness has always provided so much more than I could ever ask for."

****

Indianapolis, Indiana - 1875

They were delayed at the station in Indianapolis. It was only for a few hours, but this slight pause in their journey was long enough for Margaret to be able to run off and play. Frederick and Emma escorted her to a nearby park to allow her to run around in the grass, picking at flowers and tapping sticks along dubious looking rocks. Conversation had grown stiff and uncertain since their discussion on the train. Emma was uncertain, but it seemed as though her beloved friend was angry with her, or at the very least, upset. When little Margaret went on into the grass, laughing and playing, Emma determined that she would clear the air between them. She couldn't bear to have Frederick angry with her.

They found a bench to sit on where they could watch little Margaret from not too far a distance. The sun was out, though the air was crisp and cool, a welcoming refreshment from the staleness of the train.

"Frederick?" Emma began, hesitant.

"Hm?" was all Frederick said, more of a sound in his throat than anything else.

"I cannot help but feel as though perhaps I have upset you. If this is the case, I wish to offer my sincerest apologies. It was never my intent to cause discord between us, and I do not think I could bear it if such a dear friend were cross with me."

She put her hand along his arm before she could think better of it. He stiffened at her touch—propriety, she was certain—and she quickly pulled her hand away, feeling embarrassment color her cheeks.

"I am so sorry," she told him in a near whisper, her eyes darting out into the park to watch her little girl so that she might not have to face him. "I don't know what came over me."

Letting out a sigh, Frederick said, "I am not angry with you. I don't think I could ever be angry with you, my dear."

Shoulders slumping just a little, Emma asked without looking at him, "Then what is the matter? I must have offended you in some way."

"No, you have not offended or angered me, Emma. I'm afraid I have done this all wrong." He shook his head and took a moment to search for words. "I worry for your safety and I hope you find true happiness. This man... you do not know him, and neither do I. I worry that you are traveling so far into the unknown for the hope of something that will never be."

Frowning, Emma finally looked over at him. "You think I'm a fool, don't you?"

Taking her hands in his immediately, James explained, "No! I think you are a remarkable woman who has endured so much hardship and I admire your courage. But courage does not stop others from attempting to hurt you."

He gazed into her eyes, affection mixing there with something more intense. Something that, perhaps, had always lingered there, but she had never been able to place. Something that might be just on the verge of beautiful, waiting to spill over a floodgate that was sitting there, self-imposed.

It was not the first time he had looked at her in such a way. Many a time, Emma had felt the warmth in his gaze flittering across the air between them to wrap around her and draw her in. She felt overwhelmed by that gaze, uncertain of how to respond to it or what she should be feeling.

It was just the same now. Letting out a shaky breath,

Emma was the one to look away first, unable to handle the intensity.

"Thank you for your concern," Emma told him, her voice breathy. "But we have discussed my options before. I cannot accept your charity, however generous it is. I refuse to take advantage of a man's pity in such a way without offering anything in return. Thus, I must do what is best for my daughter. If you have no other objections, then I must ask that you no longer insist upon worrying."

Frederick continued to stare at her. Perhaps he was thinking of arguing with her, of telling her again to go back, but he knew how she felt about this particular subject. The charity of a man was acceptable only when she felt she had something to offer him in return. This man she was to meet in Montana would provide for her only because she too would provide for him, in her own way. But what did a simple woman like her have to offer Frederick?

Nothing, she thought, saddened somehow by that knowledge.

"I—" Frederick began, looking as though he was preparing himself to voice another objection, a different reasoning behind his desperate desire to have her return to Hartford. But before he could complete his thought aloud, the train sounded and Margaret came running back to the pair of them. She offered up a bouquet of lovely wildflowers to Frederick. Smiling at her, he accepted them gratefully. "They are so lovely, my darling little girl," he told her cheerfully, though Emma suspected some of it was false. "But lovely things are for lovely young women, aren't they?"

Margaret nodded and before Emma realized what he was doing, he offered her the bouquet instead. Her heart fluttered suddenly in her chest as though it was a bird trapped in too small of a cage.

She accepted the flowers with a thank you to them both, and they didn't discuss Henry, the man in Montana, for the rest of the day.

****

St. Peter, Minnesota - 1875

The Baltimore & Ohio went no further than the outlying North Western territory and wouldn't make it the rest of the way to Montana, so they needed to switch train companies in Minnesota. There was another train that went to Livingston, and that was where they would get off. Henry, the man who Emma was to marry, would take them to his home by carriage from there.

In their letters, Emma and Henry had discussed Frederick. She had explained that he was a dear old friend of her late husband, and that he insisted upon being her chaperone for her trip. In the letters, Henry had seemed unconcerned altogether about Frederick, for which Emma was relieved. She didn't know how this trip would have gone even this far without him. There were careful negotiations, however, about living arrangements before the wedding. At first, Henry was working under the assumption that Emma and her daughter would immediately be moving into his home. From what she understood of his home, it was quite large and they could each have their own room, should they choose to do so, or Emma and Margaret could share one, however they saw fit. The introduction of Frederick into the equation altered things slightly. When Emma had mentioned the presumed living arrangements to Frederick, he immediately opposed them.

"The potential for him to take advantage of the situation is entirely too great," he had told her vehemently. "You have no acquaintances in Montana; he has many. Should you need assistance to prevent from his advancements, you would be entirely without protection. No, I must insist that the living arrangements be separate until the wedding has been finalized."

Frederick's care was sweet in Emma's eyes, but she worried her suitor would be less fond of it. Carefully, she worded her response to Henry in as tactful a way as possible. She explained in simple terms first that Frederick was a very dedicated chaperone and cared for the propriety of the situation. Of course, after Henry and Emma were wed, he would be entirely acceptable of the premise of the two of them living beneath the same roof; however, in the interim, he felt it was best that they share separate quarters. It was for the sake of honesty and propriety, she had told Henry in her letter. Frederick would continue to be her chaperone right up until the day of the wedding as a means of preserving virtue and honesty.

It was a difficult letter to write—tact took so much extra time and thought than a regular letter did—and she was incredibly nervous when she had sent it off. She received a speedy reply, however, and found that Henry was amenable to the details of it. His exact words were, 'I would be disinclined to put either myself or my future wife and child in such a position as to have their virtues questioned. Your chaperone is diligent and wise.'

Emma had been relieved. Things had been shifting, however, since the beginning of their westward trip. Frederick's concern for Emma's safety and happiness had not come into question, of course, but she had begun to wonder as to his motivation behind it. Emma had always suspected that there was some kind of survivor's guilt involved, as though he somehow felt responsible for being here, alive and well, while his dear friend James had passed away. That guilt transford into a desire to support and otherwise take care of the widow and child he left behind. It was noble, in Emma's opinion, and she always felt he was a good man to do it, however, now she was beginning to wonder if there wasn't some other underlying feeling behind his desire to watch over her. She couldn't fathom what it was, until she saw him sitting with Margaret that day on the train as they were arriving at the station in Minnesota.

The two were sitting towards the window on the same side. Margaret was pointing excitedly to something which caused Frederick to laugh and nod, proceeding to explain something fascinating about the thing she was pointing to. Margaret of course didn't notice the sweet, tender look he offered to her and didn't think twice about the constant attention he often lavished on her. In her mind, Frederick had always been her favorite uncle—she had no real uncles as neither James nor Emma had any siblings—and it explained all of his affection for her. Emma didn't question it either, knowing that friendship could be as strong as blood when it came to familial ties, but as she watched them now, she realized that it was not the behavior of an uncle that she witnessed. He doted on her like a father might a daughter, as fond and loving as any man could be in that respect. Like a bolt of lightning, it struck Emma as to why he had always been so insistent to take care of the both of them. He loved little Margaret like his own daughter, not having any children of his own, and wished to continue in his affections for her. It would be much more difficult if she lived in Montana, especially with a new step-father. There was no guarantee that after Emma's union with Henry, Frederick would be allowed to be a part of Margaret's life, although Emma certainly hoped so.

When they got off the train at the St. Peter station in Minnesota, Emma clutched tightly at Margaret's hand and made sure that she followed Frederick closely. It was getting easier to keep track of each other now that they were getting used to the ways of travel, and it helped greatly that most people had long since gotten off. Only a few westbound prospectors and settlers remained on the train up to this point.

Frederick told the women to wait where their baggage was being unloaded to be sure that they retrieved all of their effects while he went to the ticket booth to confirm their plans for travel. He needed to get a carriage which would take them to the next station before the train left; if they missed it, they'd have to wait at least a day before the next one would be available.

Emma watched Frederick as he headed to the booth, thinking that he had always been quite handsome. She used to wonder why he hadn't ever married, thinking that such a wonderful man would surely have found a lovely bride by now. But he'd been disinclined to start a family; she had wondered if it didn't have something to do with his traveling, a desire for adventure perhaps, or if he simply hadn't found the right woman yet. Up until recently, she had begun to suspect that he simply didn't want the responsibility of a family. Oh, it wasn't that he would shy away from it should it fall into his lap, but she figured that he simply didn't want to give up his carefree life.

Now, as she clutched Margaret's tiny hand in hers, she thought she must have been wrong all those years. He was so careful and so sweet with Margaret, and he was always insisting on taking care of the both of them. Perhaps he now felt he was losing the closest resemblance to a family that he'd ever had.

Frowning, Emma felt a flash of guilt; she never wanted to cause Frederick pain.

After several minutes of waiting, Frederick returned to

them. "I've hailed us a carriage," he informed the both of them, speaking mainly to Emma. "The driver insists that the other train has been delayed, however, and we might have a bit of a wait. He suggested that if we hadn't yet eaten, we might find something suitable nearby."

"That sounds like an excellent idea," Emma agreed with a smile. "And perhaps we shall have time to talk?"

Frederick gave her a strange look, uncertain about what it was she wished to talk about. "Of course. I am quite sure we'll find some time for that."

Frederick and the driver did most of the loading of their luggage, both men insisting that neither Emma nor little Margaret should be helping with such heavy work. Thankfully, it was only a couple of trunks, a suitcase, and Emma's bag; Margaret kept the doll with her at all times. Frederick helped first Margaret and then Emma into the carriage before following them in himself. He'd evidently already discussed with the driver where they should be delivered, because Emma felt the carriage lurch forward as they began to move. After the rhythmic movements of the train, Emma found the carriage to be abrupt and difficult, though she made a point not to complain—she was grateful that their entire journey wasn't to be made by wagon in the first place.

"How much farther until we reach the West?" Margaret questioned, her large eyes staring up at her mother's face. She looked pale and tired, adding to the sense that she might be sickly if one didn't know of her exuberance.

"We're almost there, darling. I know it has been such a long trip, but you have done very well and I am so very proud of you."

Margaret smiled, but yawned just after that. Laying her head against her mother's lap again, she quickly fell asleep despite the jostling movements of the carriage.

For a moment, the adults in the carriage sat in silence. Emma wasn't sure if she wanted to discuss matters now or if it would be better to wait until they had more time alone.

Ultimately, all Emma managed to get out was, "Thank you for being so great with Margaret."

Frederick smiled kindly at her and replied, "I am happy that I am able to do what I can for you both."

There was more there, hanging on both their lips, but neither seemed able to address it. Silence continued until the driver pulled over finally.

"The train should be here in just two hours," he explained. "There is a small shop down the way where you can buy something to eat. Enough for a light meal anyway."

They piled their belongings on a bench at the station platform nearby. This station wasn't nearly as crowded as the previous ones; Emma suspected it was too far west to boast as many passengers. Margaret was still a little bleary from her nap on the ride to the station and yawned as she scrubbed at her eyes with tiny fists. Emma hopped her up onto the bench where she immediately leaned back and nearly fell asleep again.

"I will run to the shop," Frederick told Emma, looking at Margaret with a knowing smile. "I doubt she is in any condition to be traipsing around and I imagine neither of us are much interested in hauling all of this luggage there and back."

"Alright," Emma agreed. "But be careful and don't take too long. And, please, come back safely."

Frederick laughed a little, sounding more joyful and happy than he had for the entire trip. Bowing his head slightly in her direction, he smiled broadly and replied, "But of course. I will return with food."

After about twenty minutes, he returned, carrying a box and a glass bottle. Taking a seat beside Emma, he opened the box to reveal a loaf of bread, several small cakes, and what looked to be cups of stew. The bottle contained fresh milk to go with the small meal.

"What took you so long?" she protested, though she was mostly teasing.

"There was a terrible line," Frederick defended himself. Margaret was just waking up, and when she saw the food, she leapt up from her seat to go over to Frederick. He gave her one of the cups of stew and a hunk of the bread, promising her that she would get one of the little cakes once she was all through. Turning back to Emma, he added, "It looks as though every person waiting for this train is down at that shop ordering something for a meal. I was lucky to be as swift as I was."

He handed Emma one of the cups, which she accepted gratefully. "Thank you. I'm sorry that we couldn't sit for a real meal, but we simply cannot afford to miss this train."

Frederick waved off her apology mildly. "Of course, I completely understand. I wish you weren't in quite so big of a hurry to reach your future husband, but I understand."

Emma frowned a little as they ate. It wasn't that she was in a rush to reach Montana or Henry—the man she'd been corresponding with certainly seemed very likeable and genuine, but she didn't even know him. How could she truly feel excitement for someone she'd never met?

Perhaps a part of her was excited for the experience and for the chance at reviving her dull, unfulfilling life. She dreamed of a marriage—like her marriage to James—that might leave her breathless with a heart filled to the brim with love. But that was only a dream. In the end, the expedience of their journey had more to do with necessity and Henry's insistence. He wanted a wife very quickly, someone to build his house into a home and who might give him a blessing of children to build his own family. The desire for children had been an important factor to Emma, since she already had one of her own.

The other part of her reasoning had to do with Margaret. Her daughter had been working so hard at the sewing factory, and Emma couldn't help but feel as though each moment spent there was one less that she was spending at school.

These were all things she wanted to tell Frederick, things she felt were important to share with him, but she needed a moment alone to do so. It simply wouldn't do to tell him such things in front of Margaret.

Two hours later, they boarded the train. It was practically empty compared to the first one they picked up in Pennsylvania. This time they truly had the car all to themselves and Margaret spent several minutes flying about from one seat to the next with excitement.

Ultimately, it wasn't until much later that night that Emma finally had her moment alone with Frederick. Margaret had fallen asleep and was curled up on a seat with Frederick's coat draped over her. Frederick was staring thoughtfully out the window, and Emma took a long moment to simply watch him. He had a strong square jaw and full lips that caused dimples to appear when they pulled into a real smile, the kind where his teeth were shown. His eyes were expressive and dark, whispering of depths that went straight to his soul. His dark hair was kept short, styled carefully and deliberately.

Emma was so lost in watching him, that she didn't realize he had turned to look at her. Embarrassed, Emma looked away quickly as her cheeks burned a bright rosy red. Smiling kindly at her, Frederick said, "Is everything alright? Have I... distracted you somehow?"

"Oh, no—of course not!" she said hurriedly, shaking her head. "I merely... well, I wanted to speak with you. I was simply trying to decide what it was that I wanted to say. The last thing I'd want would be to make a fool of myself with the words I chose."

"I would hardly think you'd be capable of being a fool."

"No?" Emma found herself challenging before she could think better of it. "Isn't that how you think of me now, traveling across the country into the wildness of the West, daughter in tow, only to meet with a man I have no way of knowing with the intent of marriage?" She took a breath, realizing that her long rambling retort had been entirely inappropriate.

Frederick's eyebrows rose in surprise. "No, I don't think any such thing."

"Then why is it you're so opposed to my leaving?" Emma demanded, suddenly feeling angry as her worries began to wash over her like a tide. "Is it because of Margaret? Do you fear losing her? Because if I have any say at all, you shall always be a welcome part of my daughter's life. I would never—"

"I do fear losing Margaret, it's true," Frederick admitted, his face suddenly a mask of intensity. "But it isn't the only reason I am opposed to this endeavor. There are a thousand reasons I can think of, all of them fair and appropriate for one who acts as chaperone or friend in the capacity that I do. But they are not the one true reason for which I'd give anything I have to stop this from happening."

Searching his face as though she might find the answers there, Emma asked in a quiet voice, "Then what is your reason, Frederick?"

He hesitated. There was a long pause as silence filled

the car, making Emma wonder if he might tell her at all. Finally, after debating within himself he told her in as plain of terms as he could.

"I love you Emma. I have for so long now, I cannot even think of when it began. To see you leaving to marry another man..." He shook his head, his features shifting as though he were in pain. "I simply could not bear it."

Shock registered in Emma. It filled her up, washing through her chest and up her throat, accompanied by a full blush that seemed to warm her entire body. She couldn't think; she didn't know what to think. In love? Her dear, sweet Frederick, the friend who had stood beside her for so long as everything around her seemed to simply fall apart in a single swoop. How could this be true, and how was it that she had not noticed at all?

"I..." Emma found that she had no words. She didn't know what sort of response she should to offer him, the both of them knowing that she was currently on the train making this trip in order to meet her future husband. "I don't know what to say!"

Frederick moved from his seat across from her to kneel before her, scooping her delicate hands up in his. "I understand if there is nothing to say, my lovely Emma," he told her in a soft, deep voice that soothed an ache in her heart before she even realized it. "My timing has never been good, and I do not see why now might be any different." He laughed a little at himself, the sound sending a thrill through Emma's heart. "I was going to tell you that night in your apartment when you showed me the ad for the paper."

"Oh, Frederick, I didn't—"

He shook his head to stop her apology. "You couldn't have known. I have tried to be there for you, but you so adamantly resist my efforts. I do not begrudge you this, I only wish that it might have been different. When you told me of your desire to leave for Montana, I was heartbroken. I had waited too long to confess my love for you, and now I would never know whether or not we might have a happy life together. But you must know, that I have always loved you, Emma, and if your happiness lies in Montana, then I would take you there as fast as I could manage, no matter my own heart's expense."

As Emma thought back on all of the times Frederick had tried so diligently to take care of her and Margaret, of those moments when he would read to her daughter by the light of the fire, when he would bring them dinner without being asked and knowing that they could offer him nothing in compensation. Oh, he had always been such a good man right there in front of her, but she had never dreamed... she had never let herself even imagine that he might love her so dearly.

She hadn't dared to let herself love him.

"Frederick," she began, her heart swelling as she realized the truth that had been staring her in the face the entire time; the intensity in his eyes, the fondness in his smile. "If I had known that you loved me so, I never would have even thought to seek out another man. Frederick, you have always been so good and generous that I dared not hope that I might be so lucky twice in my life."

Hope blossomed across Frederick's features. "Emma, darling, what are you saying?"

"I'm saying that... that I love you, too."

"Oh, Emma!"

They embraced tenderly and it occurred to her then that she would have to tell her suitor that her plans had changed.

****

Livingston, Montana - 1875

When they arrived in Montana, Emma was equal parts giddy and nervous. She had found the love of her life on the train to meet her future husband and now she would have to deal with the consequences of such a realization. With Margaret in one hand and Frederick in the other, Emma felt as though she could face anything. She only hoped that Henry was as good of a man as she believed.

Henry met them at the station. He was an attractive man with strong features and hair that was only just beginning to gray. There was a beard trimmed along his jawline and brown eyes surrounded by weathered wrinkles.

"Mrs. Hammersley?"

Clearing her throat and straightening herself as best she could, she stepped forward. "Yes. Henry, I presume?"

He removed the wide brimmed hat he wore and nodded his head. "Yes, ma'am. And this is your chaperone?"

She hesitated. She had to share the truth, and the sooner the better under the circumstances.

"Yes, well he… was my chaperone," she admitted carefully. "I'm afraid that I must tell you that things have changed since the last letter you received."

Frowning, Henry glanced between Frederick and Emma. With a sigh, he said, "I think we'd best sit down and discuss this."

They spoke for nearly three hours, Emma doing most of the explaining. She told him of how she had a feeling that Frederick had been fond of her, though she had been too worried of addressing it and possibly ruining such a lovely friendship. When he finally confessed his love for her, it blossomed in her heart like a wild flower and she could never allow herself to do without him now.

Henry was less heartbroken than the average man prepared for marriage might be. He, like Emma had been herself, understood that their marriage was to be one of convenience with only the possibility of growing into something more. It meant that his feelings weren't necessarily hurt so much as the inconvenience of it all weighing itself on him.

"I understand your predicament," Henry finally told her with a sigh. "I only wish you might have found this out a bit sooner so I wouldn't have gone through the trouble of planning a wedding, you see."

Emma apologized, though she didn't know what else she might offer up in condolence. She could offer to pay for it, of course, but that seemed an unlikely situation. Frederick certainly had the money, but she wasn't about to promise his money to pay for something that was so clearly her doing.

In the end, it was Frederick who made the suggestion. "I would like to pay for the arrangements," he told Henry, sounding business like. "In return, I was wondering if perhaps we might use them so that they do not go to waste?"

Emma looked at him in surprise, but a smile quickly spread across his face. "Oh, Frederick, really?"

Smiling back at her he said, "There is nothing I would want more in this world than to have you by my side."

****

In only one week, their wedding day was set. Margaret was dressed in the most darling of little white dresses trimmed in a fine gold material that shone in the sunlight; she carried a basket of flowers which she tossed along the aisle as she moved towards where her father to be stood. Frederick looked very handsome in his suit, grey with hanging coattails and a bowtie fastened at his neck.

Irish lace woven with purple and pink flowers adorned the makeshift altar. There were only a scant few guests present—none of which Emma knew beyond Henry—but they had been invited for Henry's wedding and Emma knew they needed witnesses. She didn't mind the small venue and found it more delicate and intimate for the occasion.

When Margaret had reached the front, Emma stepped out. A quartet of violinists began to play a beautiful, soft melody as she walked down the aisle. Her beautiful, high-necked white dress dragged along the wooden clapboards as she made her way towards her betrothed. A light veil covered her face, though she could still see Frederick standing there smiling. He waited for her with baited breath until she was finally by his side. Emma stopped at the altar and handed her wildflower bouquet to her daughter, who was grinning broadly.

When she turned back to Frederick, he lifted the veil to reveal her smiling face. Taking her hands in his, the ceremony began. He promised to love her for the rest of his days and to care for her to the best of his ability. She promised to make his house a home and to love him until her last breath. When the reverend asked if they would take each other for the rest of their days, the answer was simple: "I will."

Days after the ceremony, Emma and Frederick decided

to return home to Hartford. Within the year, they were blessed with a son; another daughter followed one year later. Margaret was able to attend the best of schools, and they watched her grow into a lovely young woman—just like her mother. Emma and Frederick spent the rest of their years together, and with each passing year, they found that their love grew even stronger than ever before.

THE END

Montana Mail Order Bride Julia

Baltimore, Maryland - 1871

Julia packed up her things. She had been tending to young Marcus for nearly three weeks and now that he had passed on, it was time for her to go. There were only a few things in the Cranston household that belonged to her: clothing, a few personal mementos from her childhood, and the silver locket she'd carried with her through the war.

When she was packed, Julia hefted her large bag down the massive staircase towards the foyer. The butler, Mr. Taylor was standing at the front door awaiting her. When he saw that she was struggling with her bags, he hurried quickly up the steps to help her.

"Please, ma'am, let me take that for you," he told her, sliding his hands through the luggage straps and tugging it away from her.

She protested only a moment before accepting his kindness. "Thank you, Mr. Taylor. I think I may just miss your kindness."

He blushed a little and looked away. "Thank you, ma'am. I am sorry to see you go. House won't be the same without you."

"No, I suppose it won't."

Her mind wandered to poor little Marcus. He was only

twelve when he'd caught the pneumonia that ended up being his death. Although she had come to live with the Cranston family in order to take care of him—and with hopes that she might be able to do something for him—there were only a few in the house that she'd become fond of. Marcus, of course, who delighted in bedtime stories and hot soup, Mr. Taylor, who had taken the time to show her the ins and outs of the rather large mansion, and Miss Cora. She was twenty-five, only a year older than Julia, and was Marcus's favorite aunt. Frequently, she would skip brunch in order to play pirates with Marcus, and when he got too sick to get up from his bed, she would put on little puppet plays to entertain him.

Julia had once asked how she'd come to be so fond of the boy and Cora revealed that she could have no children of her own, making her dote lavishly upon her nephew. She was taking his death the hardest of all.

When they had reached the bottom of the stairs, Mr. Taylor put down her suitcase and turned to her. "I've hailed a carriage for you, Miss Julia," he told her somberly. "He's waiting for you outside."

Julia thanked him and gave him a quick hug, not lingering because she was still unmarried and he was a household servant. Propriety still mattered, whether she enjoyed the idea or not.

When she pulled away, Julia took one last lingering look at the mansion. It was large and, she thought, rather opulent; so different from the little apartment she had in the city. She had left it to become the live-in nurse for the Cranstons, but now that the time had come for her to leave, she was in a bit of a bad spot. She hadn't kept her apartment after moving in, thinking that there would be plenty of time to find another one before she was to leave. At the time, she had hoped her leaving would signal the return of Marcus's health rather than his death.

As things happened, Marcus died in his sleep one night, and just like that, there was no longer a need for Miss Julia.

Just as Julia was about to leave, turning towards the door as Mr. Taylor gathered up her bag once again, the door to the far room burst open. A tearful Cora glided into the room, her cheeks and nose the same rosy red color. She clutched a handkerchief and used it to dab at her eyes now and then. Sniffling, she called out to Julia, "Wait! You can't possibly leave without saying goodbye!"

Julia paused, smiling sympathetically at Cora. "I'm so sorry. I just thought it might be better for everyone if I left before the funeral service. I hate to be a bother."

Cora waved her off. "Don't be ridiculous. I consider you my dear friend. You did more for poor Marcus—" she choked a little on his name as it left her lips, "—than anyone here. I daresay you loved him more than his mother."

Sorrow plucked at Julia's heartstrings and she did her best not to grimace. She had cared for Marcus, though she had tried her best to distance herself from him. As time wore on, she knew that there was little she could do for the poor boy and death was inevitable. She didn't want him to leave such a heavy weight on her, but he had wormed his way into her gentle heart and if she were being honest with herself, his death affected her greatly.

"I will miss him," she answered Cora in a small voice.

Cora sniffled as she came to a halt in front of Julia. "Oh, I don't want to stay in this house with its dreadful ghosts!"

Julia understood that this wasn't just about Marcus. Cora and her family had experienced a good deal of grief the last few years—many people had after the war with the South—and more than a few hard memories wandered the mansion halls.

Taking Cora's hand in her own, Julia gave it a gentle squeeze in comfort. "You won't stay, will you?"

Cora shook her head. "No. Christian and I are going to New York in a few days. My brother-in-law is already unhappy with my extended stay and he and Christian have never gotten along."

"Perhaps that is for the best. There's nothing really keeping you here now."

With a sigh, Cora nodded her head in agreement. "No, there isn't. My sister is too busy worrying over her dresses and the state of the house to even acknowledge her grief, and I am not interested in enduring the inevitable argument between the two of us because of it." Dabbing at her eyes and sniffling again, Cora asked, "And what of you? Where shall you go now that my dear nephew has left for Heaven?"

"I have an uncle in New Haven," Julia explained with only a hint of embarrassment. She wasn't too keen on traveling to New Haven and even less so to stay with her uncle. He was a stout man, strict and on occasion, cruel. There was fairness in him, but it came in short bursts that left everyone around him uneasy. "I'll be taking the train there tonight so that I can stay with him."

Cora's expression was one of surprise. "Oh! I hadn't realized you would be leaving the state entirely. And to the North, no less!"

Julia ignored the comment of the North. The war was over and there were no longer the Union and the Confederacy; they were all one nation now. Maryland had been the southernmost Union state, meaning that much of its population had been divided on the opinion. There were some, like Cora and her family, who had thought they ought to have been Confederates, and maybe in their hearts were. Julia, however, had been a nurse's assistant in the war. She was only seventeen, hardly old enough for much of anything, but when they called for volunteers to help out the wounded soldiers, she had eagerly offered. It had taught her an awful lot, including how to be a nurse, her current profession. She believed in the Union and trusted it to pull them through the terrible times ahead.

"I'm afraid I'm in a bit of a spot," Julia admitted to her friend. "Since moving in here, I had lost my old apartment in the city. I thought I might have enough time to get a new one, but my search has been fruitless." She shook her head with a sigh of dejection. "My uncle is kind enough to offer me shelter, for a time."

Perhaps it was the way Julia said "kind" or maybe it was simply the situation all itself, but Cora frowned and began to shake her head. "No, no. That simply won't do at all." Snapping her fingers to get Mr. Taylor's attention, she said to him, "Tell the driver to go ahead. We won't be needing his assistance."

"Yes, ma'am."

Bewildered, Julia didn't even get the chance to tell Mr. Taylor not to do that before he was running out to the driver. Whirling back on Cora in disbelief, she said, "Now why would you do that! I must leave soon or I'll miss my train!"

"You're not taking the train," Cora told her, linking their arms together and steering her towards a back room. "You're staying with me and Christian until such time as you have found a suitable new living arrangement."

"I can't do that!" Julia protested; she didn't enjoy receiving charity.

Cora ignored her and continued. "I'll help you to find a

new apartment—or even better, a husband!"

****

Christian was making small talk with Mary's husband Charles in the other room, likely sipping brandy, leaving the women alone in the sitting room. Mary, Cora's sister and the late Marcus's mother, was dressed all in black, much like Cora, and held a teacup in her delicate hands, though she hadn't taken a sip from it in a long while. Julia was there only by the grace and goodness of Cora, who had insisted she stay, despite Julia's reluctance. They had written to her uncle and explained that Julia would not be taking advantage of his generosity at this time, leaving her free to pursue other avenues.

That was the topic of discussion that night: other avenues.

"I think it's a brilliant idea!" Cora exclaimed, beaming so that she looked almost comical in her mourning attire. It was at odds with everything else at the moment, but a smile was a welcome change at the very least.

Julia shook her head. She was wearing black as well, though it was hardly required, but it was of a much plainer thread and design than that of the other women. They came from families of wealth and married into similar families; Julia was middle class at best.

"I really don't know, Miss Cora," Julia replied hesitantly. She didn't want to upset her generous hostess, but at the same time she couldn't help but balk at her suggestion. "So many of those listings are by con men."

Cora waved her off. "Nonsense. I found my husband through a Matrimonial ad!"

"Cora, really," Mary interrupted, sounding bored instead of grief-stricken as she should have been. "I hardly think your marriage is the flame by which all candles should be compared."

Cora sent her a rueful look, wagging her finger at her

sister. "Now you see here, Mary! Christian has been a wonderful husband and I am quite happy to have found him! What more should I expect from a marriage?"

"Stability? A man who is less eager for travel and more eager for making contacts and acquaintances that will further the family's worth?"

"Oh, don't be ridiculous! That's what your marriage is for."

The women continued to argue for a while longer, but Julia was hardly paying attention. She was giving Cora's suggestion some very serious thought and was beginning to think that perhaps it wasn't so ludicrous as she initially thought. Although she doubted that she would be so lucky as to find a man that she loved as Cora had, there was a good chance that she might find a man who could take care of her.

She was still mulling it over in her mind, but the idea was planted like a seed and she wasn't ready to dismiss it just yet.

"Miss Cora, how might I go about finding a match?"

The two women stopped arguing abruptly and Cora smiled broadly at her friend; her sister rolled her eyes in boredom.

****

Julia felt a little foolish to be searching the newspaper for something that should have been such a personal thing. Ever since she was a girl, she had dreamed of the day she might marry a handsome young man who would spend the rest of his days devoted to her. Of course, as she had grown older and seen even a fraction of the horrors that war provided, she grew to understand that she had been a little naïve for such hopes. Even so, she'd kept them snuggled away in her heart, protected and coveted until the day she might marry.

The newspaper felt incredibly impersonal to Julia; she didn't care for the idea of finding her husband before ever meeting him. But there was Cora, along with many other young women, who had done just this and ended up incredibly happy. Julia wasn't sure if she could be so lucky, but as she stared at the paper settled on the table in front of her, she determined that perhaps it was worth a shot after all. Besides, the alternative was even less inviting than the idea of marrying a stranger. Biting her lip, Julia had managed to talk herself into the endeavor all over again. Anything was better than her uncle's house, wasn't it?

Scooping up the paper, she opened it up to the section that contained the personal ads. There were several different kinds, many calling for maids, cooks, or tutors—she was nearly sidetracked by these, thinking perhaps they were more reasonable—but on the second page, she found what she was looking for. Matrimonials.

Her eyes landed on the first one and read through it quickly.

MATRIMONIAL – Fifty-three-year-old wealthy bachelor in search of young country girl. Must have no education and a base nature. Easily teachable in the ways, duties, and expectations of a woman.

Julia's eyes went wide and she couldn't help the sudden shudder than ran through her. Perhaps she was merely misinterpreting the thing, but she couldn't help but feel as though the ad was calling for a young girl to turn towards prostitution! A base nature indeed! The ad all but begged for an innocent youth with the promise of corrupting her. It was grotesque enough that Julia nearly gave up her search after it had only just begun, determining that she wanted no part of such debauchery.

But after a steadying breath, she carefully convinced herself that she had misread the ad's meaning—and she promptly went on to the next one—searching once more for something suitable to herself.

The next one seemed far less offensive and worrisome to her delicate sensibilities.

MATRIMONIAL – Thirty-eight-year-old homesteader in search of a marriageable woman between the ages of sixteen and forty. Must be able to cook, clean, and milk a cow. Must also be wealthy in her own right. I request no poor women respond.

Julia sighed as she read the last part. She had little doubt that she could learn to milk a cow as the ad requested, but she was most certainly not independently wealthy by any stretch of the imagination. This was the type of ad Cora might respond to as she had the money to do as she pleased with or without the assistance of outside funds. Though, to be honest, Julia had to laugh at the idea of Cora milking a cow or anything of the like, perhaps on some large cattle ranch out West, working and cleaning for a prospector in search of gold. It was as ridiculous as it was improbable. Cora wasn't the type to do her own labor if she could help it; she had the money that she could help it.

Still smiling, Julia moved on to the next ad; she was without much hope, but was still willing to try.

MATRIMONIAL – Thirty-year-old widower in search of respectable young woman in regards to marriage. Must be family oriented and will to help raise a young boy of an inquisitive and adventurous nature. Please do not respond idly.

Julia stared at that one a long while. It was very perfunctory and to the point. There was no passion to it; there was no intrigue. But she felt compelled to read it again and again, maybe even a dozen times. She didn't know what drew her to it, but she got up to retrieve a piece of paper and an envelope quickly from the drawing room. There was an address listed just below the ad and before she had even truly decided to do it, she had scribbled it down on the back of the envelope. Putting it and the newspaper aside, she pulled the paper to her.

'To the Concerned Party,' she wrote, realizing that there was no name listed in the ad. Pressing forward anyway, she scribbled a very brief letter denoting her interest in his posting.

I have experience in tending to young children and as of yet am unmarried. In the interest of honesty, I must also confess that I have little money of my own. If my response is undesirable, please send a brief reply to dismiss my interest.

She signed her name easily and folded up the letter, quickly stuffing it inside the envelope before she could reconsider her perhaps foolish reply. The next day she would mail it, she promised herself, and in the meantime, she would continue to search the papers for similar ads.

She had decided that this was the best way after all and she wanted additional options should this one fall through.

It wasn't for love; this was all business now.

****

It was nearly three weeks since Julia had sent out her letter. So much time had passed that she had decided that she wasn't going to get an answer at all from that first ad she responded to. Since then, she had mailed off a dozen letters, and there were more still that she was sifting through carefully in hopes of making a smart match for herself. She was attempting to move as quickly as possible, hoping that she might find a suitable ad with a suitable husband at the other end of it.

Cora and her husband had put off their trip to New York; Julia knew it was because of her. Mary and her husband were quickly growing irate with Julia's continued presence, though she did her very best to stay out of their way. Mary would send her dirty glances and then when she was caught, would turn up her nose and whisper to whomsoever might be in the room, "She is a reminder of my poor son! Haven't I suffered enough already?" When her sister was in the room, she would hiss it at her maliciously and the fight would begin as it inevitably always did.

All of this made Julia search more earnestly for a means of leaving this place. She was fond of Cora's friendship and hoped that they might stay friends whatever her future might hold, but she had no desire to remain in the cold mansion.

Cora was the type of woman who would never insist that Julia leave; she was a guest here. But Julia was growing uneasy about the whole thing as time pressed on and urgency began to nag at her. It didn't help that the house reminded her so much of dear Marcus. She hadn't wanted to admit it to herself, but his death had left a swell of grief to fill her heart and it slowly ate away at her.

Just as Julia was preparing another letter inquiring to an

ad—this one more of a governess position than anything else—a letter came for her. It was longer than the one she had written to begin with, but the scrawl was quick and deliberate all the same.

Miss Julia,

Your reply is welcome. I encourage you to join me in Montana. I shall pay for your ticket; it is enclosed below. Perhaps that is presumptuous on my part, but I am an impatient man and have no desire to wait. Should you still wish to answer my ad, I ask only that you use the ticket provided as I require no answering letter be it yes or no. But I must also ask you to finish reading this letter before you make your decision.

I have placed this ad for the sake of my eight-year-old son. His mother—God rest her sweet soul—has passed on and I worry about his development as a young lad. Grief has stricken him quite strongly. He needs a mother and to that end, I placed this ad. I am not searching for a personal companion or for love; I have had these things already. To ask for them again would be selfish.

If you are in search of love, I must ask that you reconsider your interest to protect your assumed gentle heart.

I make this promise to you, should you choose to venture to my Montana home anyway: I will always take care of you. I will provide for you. You shall want for nothing. But I cannot give you love, not as a man loves his wife. Perhaps we might come to an arrangement of mutual sympathies and friendship, but even that I cannot promise.

I shall look for you on the train. If you are not there, then I must assume that these terms are not agreeable or suitable to your long-term goals and that I have scared you off.

Best,

Wyatt Baroque

Julia stared at the letter for a long time. The penmanship was quite beautiful; elegant loops and fluid lines covered the page. The letter was rather unflattering and was clearly meant to be firm, strict, and perhaps even unwelcoming, Julia thought. But it didn't leave her with that sentiment at all. She felt no menace from his words; she felt only grief. Perhaps it was her own quiet despair over Marcus's death; maybe it was the pressure she felt to leave. Either way, Mr. Baroque's letter left her only with a profound sense of sadness.

She couldn't be sure, but Julia felt that this was what reinforced her own resolve. She would go to him and perhaps there, she could forget the death that hovered so near to her own heart.

****

Cora escorted Julia to the train station. She insisted on paying for the carriage, since the ticket for the train was already covered by Julia's wealthy husband to be.

"That's an excellent sign!" Cora explained brightly. "The hustlers and the rakes are always insisting that you send them money. If he's already paying your way to him, it must mean that he has money!"

Julia nodded. She was being quiet, even more so than usual today. Her nerves had started to get the better of her, leaving her with a sense of dread and foreboding. She had committed to this decision and she stood by that even now, but it did nothing to ease her apprehension. The man had made it clear that this was not for the purpose of love. Could Julia live with that?

She had, of course, decided that she could and thus had made her way to the train station in order to meet him, but part of her was still wistful for that girlhood dream of romance and love. Still, an arrangement of convenience wasn't something she could afford to turn her nose down to.

"Oh, he must be crazy about you!" Cora gushed, motioning for the young man who had come with the carriage driver to follow them. He was carrying Julia's bag for her; she was grateful all of a sudden that she had so little to call her own. "You must write quite a letter! It took at least a dozen correspondences, three letters to my parents, and one awful dinner with my sister before Christian and I made such a connection."

Julia hadn't explained the situation to her friend, fearing that she might disapprove and attempt to talk Julia out of it. She couldn't afford something like that and she was unwilling to allow Cora to delay her own plans for the sake of Julia's misfortune. After all, Cora wanted to leave that mansion, perhaps just as badly as Julia did, and the only thing preventing her from making the trip to New York with her husband was that Julia was as of yet unsettled.

How could she worry her dear friend then after all she had done for her? And besides, Julia didn't feel that Mr. Baroque was a dangerous man. He merely seemed overly practical and perhaps a little shrewd. The type of man that broached no rebellion or discord from those around him. That didn't make him a bad man, though it would likely make him difficult to live with. And in his letter, though he could not promise her love, he did say there was the possibility for friendship to blossom. Surely that was enough of a reason for Julia to push forward.

She doubted very much she would find anything better.

"You didn't tell me his name," Cora chided as they headed along the station. The train wasn't yet boarding so they had a few minutes still before they would have to part.

"Mr. Wyatt Baroque," Julia answered in a small voice, trying to hide her apprehension.

She needn't have worried, of course, because Cora was too excited over the whole thing to be worried with the minute details of Julia's person.

"Ooh, that is a nice name," Cora said, eyes glittering. "It has the strength of the West, but the culture of the East! I'm sure you've won yourself quite a prize."

Julia smiled at her friend and nodded. "I think you are right." It was a bit of a lie, but Julia hoped that maybe it would be true when she arrived.

If nothing else, I shall be forever taken care of, Julia thought, trying to remember her reasoning for accepting his decisively quick offer.

"Of course I am!" Cora told her quickly. The whistle

sounded loudly and the man at the entrance to the train called for all passengers to board. Cora escorted Julia the rest of the way, speaking urgently. "Now, be sure that you write me as soon as you arrive there in Montana. If your wedding date is to be set for later, please, send word and I shall make sure that both myself and Christian shall attend. My sister, thankfully, will not of course. Now, should the wedding be immediate, of course it is highly unlikely that I shall have the time to make arrangements to attend. Oh, perhaps I should just come with you now!"

Cora had been toying with the idea of escorting Julia to Montana since she learned that Julia had indeed found herself a suitable match. Julia, of course, had talked her out of it half a dozen times already. How would she explain that to Mr. Baroque? How would she explain the situation to Cora once they arrived? No, it simply would not do to have Cora come with her, although she would in a sense be a comfort to have with her on the journey. She was traveling to an entirely new place in what many still referred to as the Wild West. Having a companion who had her interests at heart would bring her at least some peace of mind, but Julia simply couldn't accept the cost of that.

No, she had to do this on her own and was determined to do just that.

"Miss Cora, we've been over this already," Julia reminded her. "I would be most happy to correspond with you via letter, but I hardly think it appropriate to bring a lady friend of mine when I am only just now meeting my future husband. I think it is only right that we are allowed time to become better acquainted before we are to worry about friends interfering."

Cora looked a little put out by this, but didn't argue. She surely knew that Julia was correct in her assessment, even if it wasn't the only reason she was so against Cora attending.

"I do wish you at least had a chaperone!" Cora protested, looking up at the man who was now checking boarding passes of those getting on the train. "Even if your future husband is a wonderful man, there are so many dangerous people on trains these days! I prefer a good old carriage, myself, but Christian insists that it is the wave of the future. Progress, he calls it."

She made a wave of her hand as though this was ridiculous. Cora wasn't one for progress, preferring the way things were instead. She enjoyed the comfort and kindness of routine, of things staying the same. Julia preferred the promise of the new and the adventurous, although the war had quelled at least some of that.

Finally, it was time for Julia to go. There was no more time for dallying or talking or anything of the sort. This was the last call for boarding passengers.

Looking a little teary eyed, Cora embraced her friend tightly. In her ear, she whispered, "Oh my dear Julia! Write me soon and give word of how you are doing. You have both my address here and in New York. Use them both as you must!"

With that, they parted ways, Julia boarding the train that would speed her away towards her new life.

****

Livingston, Montana - 1871

Julia arrived at the station in Montana early that morning. It was brisk and cool, just barely turning from winter to spring, and with the sun still so low on the horizon, she could still see the fog of her breath as she left the train. Once on the platform, Julia retrieved her single bag and began to search the many faces there. She had no idea what Mr. Baroque looked like, knowing only that he was a thirty-year-old widower. He had a son also, but she was unsure whether or not the son might be present as well.

There were a good many faces there on the platform, either waiting to board and leave Montana, or waiting for those disembarking the train. Most of the passengers were men, so perhaps she would at least be easier to spot, but it seemed as though all of those waiting were men as well. They wore thick, long brown coats and wide brimmed hats, and most had beards that varied in color from brown to gray to a golden red. How was she supposed to find Mr. Baroque in a sea of so many possibilities?

Clutching her bag, Julia began to look around. She would have to start asking people, she decided, if she was going to find him. The first man she came upon seemed a little too old, with wisps of gray in his beard.

"Excuse me, sir?" she asked as politely as she could.

He turned to look at her, his eyes squinting and beady, but inspecting her with a shrewd gaze. "Ma'am?"

"I am looking for a Mr. Baroque. Might you have seen him?"

His bushy eyebrows rose in surprise and he took a step back, examining her once again, more carefully this time. "Whatcha need with Mr. Baroque?"

A quiet blush crept up along her cheeks, making them feel warm despite the cool air. Did she tell this man the truth? Was this the type of thing men out West might discuss? Cora had obviously shared her personal experiences with the whole thing, but that didn't speak as to whether or not Christian felt comfortable talking about the arrangement.

Finally, Julia cleared her throat and answered, "I am here to take care of his young son." It was both honest and discreet, she felt.

"I see," said the man. "Well, then I might take you right on to him then, ma'am. I'm Mr. Clemens, his business partner."

They shook hands and Julia introduced herself. They didn't discuss much after that, Julia preferring not to openly talk about the arrangement with Mr. Baroque until she knew where he stood on it, and Mr. Clemens evidently preferring silence to idle chit chat.

Mr. Clemens escorted Julia to the far side of the platform. Again, there were so many people waiting that it hardly seemed possible that she might be able to pick out Mr. Baroque from any of them. It was pure luck that she had come across Mr. Clemens, such a helpful older man who knew Mr. Baroque.

When they reached a bench, Julia saw a young man sitting there with a newspaper held out so that he might read. He was handsome with defined features and a short, smart haircut. Hope surged within Julia as she thought perhaps this was him.

"May I introduce Mr. Wyatt Baroque," Mr. Clemens said, but it wasn't the sitting man he gestured towards.

Next to the bench was another man, standing. He, too, was attractive, if maybe a little more worn than the man beside him. He wore a dark suit and a heavy brown overcoat that stopped just below his knees. He wore no hat; his coppery red hair was combed back tidily and his matching beard was kept trim and light. Although he was less typically handsome and seemed just a little rough around the edges, despite his sharp suit and his deliberately combed hair, Julia found herself still quite impressed with his appearance.

His eyes were blue and they searched her just as shrewdly as Mr. Clemens had.

"Hank, it seems you've found my future wife."

****

Mr. Baroque escorted Julia to his carriage drawn by two incredibly lovely black horses who seemed to enjoy carrot sticks immensely. He drove himself and told Julia to sit inside the cab where it was warmer. She didn't protest, uncertain of what she might say in way of conversation should she choose to ride with him anyway, and found herself grateful for the small protection from the elements once she was settled inside.

As the carriage began to move, it grew increasingly bumpy. The train ride had been relatively smooth, although the chugging of the engine and the tooting of the horn hardly made it relaxing. There had been plenty of movement, of course, but most of it had been a consistent swaying back and forth rather than the bumping and pitching of the carriage. Even so, it had been a long trip; Julia was tired. She spent a good deal of her time watching outside through the windows, seeing the buildings coming up around Livingston until they became fewer and fewer. Soon, there was little more than trees and the open range than signaled the plains of the area. Still, they pressed on.

After a time, despite her intentions, Julia felt her eyelids droop heavily and her attentions wander. Before she had even realized what had happened, she was fast asleep, her head leaning against the door.

It wasn't until the carriage jerked to a halt, that Julia awoke again. The sudden stop caused her to fall forward slightly and she only just caught herself, the fall waking her abruptly.

Shaking the sleep from her body, Julia looked outside once again. They had stopped outside of a large mansion, as big as any Julia had ever seen. But it wasn't like the mansions in the East. It was two story, of course, with the same white washed facing and tall pillars and a large porch for sitting. Beyond the house, however, was a noticeable fence keeping in cattle and horses alike. It was a ranch with plenty of land and huge beasts of burden that were both impressive and beautiful.

Julia stared in awe at the property. She was so lost in the beauty and size of it, that she didn't notice Mr. Baroque until he was opening the door for her and had brought out a small crate to make her descent a little easier.

"This entire place belongs to you?" Julia asked, unable to hide her awe.

Mr. Baroque nodded. Thus far, he had not yet smiled at her even once, and while he remained cordial to a T, he was most definitely not a welcoming man. He didn't make her feel uncomfortable, but he made no bones about her purpose there.

Julia climbed out of the carriage and accepted his hand to help her down. "Will you show me the area?" she inquired hesitantly, not sure if this might be crossing one of those boundaries he insisted would be erected immediately upon her arrival.

Mr. Baroque didn't say anything for a long moment. He reached for her bag and began escorting her towards the front door of the mansion, a thoughtful frown on his face. When he finally said anything in response, they were in front of the door. "I will give you a proper tour of the property, yes. As I have explained, this will be your home and I intend to make your stay here as pleasant as possible. There will be some matters that should be discussed additionally, and I would prefer my son not be present for them until we have gone over them as adults."

Julia nodded. She had been so distracted by Mr. Baroque—both his uniquely handsome appearance and his aloof mannerisms—that she had all but forgotten about the young boy who would be her charge for the years that followed. Eagerness bloomed in her chest; she wanted very much to meet the young man.

"Shall I meet him first?" she asked, trying to taper her eagerness but failing. She couldn't help but find that she wanted so very much to fill the empty hole young Marcus had left in his wake.

Mr. Baroque glanced at her in surprise, his eyebrows lifted slightly to make his beautiful blue eyes all the more noticeable and impressive. "No. Not today," he answered after a moment, opening the door. Julia felt her heart drop suddenly. "I thought it best he be tutored until such times as I could find either a suitable wife or a suitable governess."

"And which am I?" Julia asked before she could stop herself. It was a silly question and deliberately provocative. She knew exactly where she stood on the matter; it had been made perfectly clear to her the details of her arrangement in his letter before she arrived.

Mr. Baroque turned to fix her with a piercing stare, one that was probably meant to be stern—even menacing—but instead, it only entranced Julia. She found herself searching those deep, soulful eyes in hopes of finding the truth within them. They didn't look like the eyes of a dangerous man or an angry man. They only looked like they were in pain.

"Don't sass me, Miss Julia," he told her sternly, but his eyes remained as they were, incapable of any real anger. "I expressed my intentions very clearly in my letter to you and I told you then that if you had any misgivings on the matter, then you ought not to show up at all. If you are having them now, then perhaps I had best take you back to the station and buy you another ticket home."

Julia met Mr. Baroque's gaze evenly; she wasn't afraid.

His words stung a little bit more than she had thought they would. He was correct, of course, this entire arrangement was one of convenience and to challenge it already as though she might be desirous of something more, something he couldn't provide and had expressed early on that he couldn't, seemed unfair all of a sudden.

Looking away finally, she apologized. "I don't know what came over me," she told him sincerely. "I understand the arrangement and I meant no disrespect. I'm sure that I will learn to acclimate to the situation perfectly, given only a little bit of time."

He looked uncertain, but gave her a single nod in agreement. Then he pushed open the door and escorted her inside. The mansion was beautiful, extending like a ballroom as soon as they stepped through the door. It was a foyer, but connected to the sitting room and the living room, which were separated only by a long wall that stopped short of the foyer. There was a staircase to her immediate left which obviously went to the second story and opened up to a hallway that overlooked the first floor. Paintings lined the walls, many of them depicting severe looking people in fine clothing. Others were less structured, showing a family running through an orchard and a young maid milking a goat. They each had ornate frames polished in gold and copper colors.

"The ground floor contains the living room, the sitting room, the music room, and the kitchen. There is also the sun room off the east side of the house." Mr. Baroque escorted her through the house, pointing out each of the rooms, always being polite and descriptive, but hardly granting her more than a passing glance. When he'd escorted her to the back of the house where the kitchen and the mud room were, they looped back around going through the sun room.

Julia's lips parted as they entered, wonder lighting her eyes as she saw the glass windows that ran from the floor to the ceiling. The entire room was designed like a pentagon, three of the five sides made entirely of glass, while the last two were attached to the back wall of the house. Light flooded the room, making it easily the brightest room of the house. The floors were a hard, light colored wood that echoed beneath their feet as they walked through it. There were curtains pulled to the side of each of the large windows; they were an airy, faint white that was all but transparent. There were only a few pieces of furniture in the room, the rest of it otherwise unused and open. A chaise lounge chair was settled in the middle of the room, the cushions a pale pink with delicate blue flowers embroidered on them, and a golden-brown framework that shone against the light. There was also a small table for coffee or tea, a second chair, several pillows pushed off to the side, and a trunk that was settled against the wall.

"It's beautiful," Julia told Mr. Baroque breathlessly. "I would think this might be my favorite room in the house."

He didn't say anything for so long that Julia finally glanced over at him, only to find that he was staring at her strangely. There was a soft expression on his face that disappeared as soon as he caught her watching. Coughing into his hand, he cleared his throat and said, "Shall we visit the upstairs?"

Julia only nodded, still wondering what that look had meant.

The upstairs was equally beautiful and very tastefully done. Julia was shone where her quarters would be—they would share separate accommodations until the wedding and afterwards they could discuss other arrangements, he told her. The room was lovely, of course, decorated with a woman in mind. The duvet was a pearly white color with a light blue trim and green embellishments. Several pillows were piled on the bed as well, matching in color and design, and an additional fleece blanket was folded up at the end of the bed. There was a vanity, a bookcase—mostly with knickknacks as opposed to actual books—and an armoire made of beautiful stained cherrywood.

"I trust that this room will be to your liking," Mr. Baroque told her briskly. "If it is not, let me know of what changes need to be made and I shall have them done immediately."

Julia thanked him, but said that she had no need to change any of it. As they turned away, she contemplated the bookshelf. "I do have one request," she amended as they left her room.

He hmm'd in answer.

"Might I have books? I enjoy reading on medicine as well as having something for your young boy to read. A healthy mind makes a healthy boy."

Mr. Baroque glanced back at her as they made their way down the hall to the other rooms. He considered her thoughtfully for a moment before he nodded. "Very well. Whatever material is to your liking."

Later that day, when Julia was settled—she had very little to unpack—she heard a commotion just down the stairs. She had been up in her room but at the sudden bursting open of the door and sharp cries, she hurried down the stairs to see what was the matter.

When she reached the first floor, however, she found that nothing was wrong at all.

Mr. Baroque had caught a small boy up in his arms and was smiling broadly as he swung him around through the air. They laughed and spun for several long moments before stopping abruptly at the sight of Julia standing there.

Clearing his throat, Mr. Baroque put the child down on the ground again and introduced him to Julia. "Son, this is Miss Julia. She is going to be your new mother."

The boy shied away from her, though she did her best to smile in a friendly matter, and clung to his father's leg.

"Miss Julia, this is my son, John. You must forgive his shyness; he is only eight."

"Of course," Julia said easily. She knelt down so that she was eye level with the boy and said in a stage whisper, "I'm quite nervous around new people as well. I was hoping that you might be brave and make it easier on me."

The soft tenor of her voice and her plea for assistance seemed to bring the boy out, only a little, but enough that he offered her his hand. She smiled as she shook it lightly.

"Don't worry Miss Julia," he said. "My dad's not scary at all."

At this, Julia laughed. "No, he isn't." Looking up at Mr. Baroque she added in a softer tone, "Not at all."

****

It was nearly a month after moving to Montana that Julia began to realize it. They had been married only two days after her arrival, just enough time for John to warm slightly to the idea of having her around, and since then, she had continued to remain in her own room. Her feelings on the situation had changed without her meaning them to. It was due to small things: brief touches of the hand as they passed books, cups or coats between them; lingering glances on the spring nights that were growing longer every day; a soft word from his lips. Julia had understood when she answered the ad that love was not what Mr. Baroque—Wyatt—was looking for. He merely wanted a caregiver for his eight-year-old son, John. But now Julia was finding that love happened anyway—on her part. That was the problem, though; Wyatt remained unchanged in his position on their marriage.

Julia tried to occupy herself by spending time with John. He was a precocious little child, always eager to learn and to test his imagination and his limits. She found that she very much enjoyed his company, though he reminded her almost painfully of her dear, sickly Marcus. She took to reading to him in the sun room, taking advantage of the early mornings and the extended afternoons, basking in the golden sunlight that filled the room. As per their agreement, Julia would tell Wyatt of the books she wanted and he would ensure they arrived as quickly as possible. It meant that she had a multitude of children's tales to share with John.

Some days they would spend the afternoon acting out the storybooks, dueling like pirates or dancing around like princes and princesses. Other days, John would simply sit on Julia's lap and allow her to read the story out loud to him. He was a quick learner, very smart, and so interested in the world that he would often ask her to read more advanced things, like books on the natural world. She was all too happy to oblige.

His interest made him a handful on occasion. Some days he would stare out the windows as they were sitting down for reading time, not paying attention at all. She would scold him, but only a little. Julia understood that he was just a boy of eight and that being outside was as important as the things he would read in a book for his development. That was why she allowed him outside to play on days instead of reading, though not every day, and always with supervision.

One of Julia's duties on the ranch was making meals. She had discussed it with Mr. Baroque, who had offered to hire her a cook and a maid if she required them, and decided that she wanted to take care of the household on her own. Once a week, a woman from town would come in a help out with things that Julia had fallen behind on, but otherwise, the house was hers.

This was why little John was outside on his own, playing amidst the horses. She had told him not twenty minutes earlier that she had to make lunch for them and his father; he was to find something entertaining to occupy himself with inside the house until she was done. Being the adventurous little boy he was, he disregarded her wishes and bound out of the house, sneaking past his father in the sitting room, and raced to the wide expansive land that made up the ranch.

Julia was just finishing up lunch when she heard the cry. It sounded like it was John.

Dropping the dish immediately, she rushed to the front. Wyatt was there as well, having heard the same noise as she had. "Where is John?" she asked him, feeling panic bubbling up within her breast.

Instead of answering, Wyatt raced outside, Julia hot on his heels. There was another cry, and this time, Julia was positive it was John.

She spotted him a moment later. He was lying in the dirt, body turned around awkwardly. Holding his leg, he cried and called for help. In the distance, Julia could just see a young colt bucking and tossing his mane.

"John!" she cried, racing towards him. Wyatt had seen him, too, and they reached the boy at the same time.

"John, my boy, are you alright?" asked Wyatt, reaching for his son.

"No!" warned Julia, stopping Wyatt who looked as though he was ready to scoop his son up into his arms. "Look at his leg!"

Wyatt glanced down at the leg John was clutching at; it was bent at an abnormal angle.

"I think it's broken. Moving him may make it worse. We need to set it before we can do anything else."

John was crying, calling for his father, and Wyatt looked as though he wanted to disregard all of Julia's words and take him immediately to the doctor. But he didn't. Instead, he went around behind his son and lifted him ever so slightly by the shoulders; the boy wailed.

"Shhh," Wyatt told him gently, easing his son's head into his lap. "You're going to be just fine, son."

Wyatt looked up at Julia, as though asking if he was lying to his little boy. Julia gave him a curt nod and said, "That's right. You'll be just fine. But I need you to be brave and wait here with your father for just a moment. We need to set your leg before it gets worse, and I need a few things in order to do that."

John sniffled, looking as though he was ready to burst into tears once more, but his father was near and it lent him the courage to nod.

Wyatt's gaze locked with Julia's for a moment and she saw the worry there, the tenderness and the love for his son. "Hurry," was all he said to her.

Julia wasted no time. She hurried back to the house to grab what she needed: several lengths of clean linen, two long, but thin boards that were sturdy, and a piece of chocolate. There was nothing she could do for the pain, but at least she could boost his sugar levels. Within minutes, Julia had returned, arms full of supplies. John was looking pale, his pain mitigated by his father's presence, but Julia knew that wouldn't do much for him.

"Alright, John, I'm going to need you to be a brave boy," she told him in her sweetest voice. "I know this hurts terribly, but you're so strong and we're going to do our best to make this better, okay?"

John nodded his head; he didn't look excited for whatever Julia was about to do.

Placing her materials to the side, she laid out the solid boards next to John's leg, making sure that they wouldn't be too long to use. They were longer than his calf, stretching past his knee, which was good; he wouldn't be able to bend his leg. She had them ready, knowing that she was going to have to move quickly once she started.

"What are you going to do?" Wyatt asked. His voice was calm as was his expression, but Julia was starting to learn about Wyatt. Although he could keep his tone and his muscles cool and unaffected, his eyes were indeed the window to his soul. They spoke volumes while the rest of him was all but silent. The result left him with a tell only those who took the time to stare into his eyes would see. People like Julia.

Julia remained chipper as she answered Wyatt, trying to keep John calm; she knew he wouldn't appreciate what was to come next. "I'm going to straighten this out and set it so that he heals right as rain."

Wyatt paled ever so slightly and the corners of his eyes tightened, letting Julia know that he understood what she was preparing to do. The fact that he made no protest or movement to stop her told her that he was willing to trust her enough to do this.

Smiling down at John, Julia told him, "On the count of three."

He nodded as his father gripped him tightly, holding him down in preparation for what was to come next. "Okay," said John.

But Julia only got to one when she gripped little John's ankle and jerked his leg outward. The little boy cried out in agony at the pain of it, but surprise had dulled the sensation slightly. He stared at her, wide eyed and disbelieving. "You said three!" he cried out, but his voice wasn't strong and he was so pale. Before Julia even had the chance to answer him, he fainted in his father's arms.

Julia was relieved; it would give her the chance to set the leg without causing him additional pain. She worked in silence and wrapped it up quickly. When she'd tied the wrappings around his leg and the boards, holding it in place, Wyatt finally lifted him up in his arms and together they went back to the house. Neither of them said anything until Wyatt had tucked his son into bed and they were both back downstairs.

Julia was shaking with nervous energy, feeling the danger of what had just happened and hoped with all her heart that John would be fine. He had to be fine. Needing to do something, Julia returned to the kitchen and began to clean up the mess she'd made when she dropped the lunch she had been preparing earlier. Wyatt had followed her to the kitchen and for a long moment stood in the doorway, silently watching.

"He'll be on the mend for at least eight weeks; maybe longer," Julia began speaking to him, but never looked up from what she was doing. "You should give him the chocolate when he wakes; the sugar will help. He's a good boy and very strong. I think he's too determined to let this keep him down for long. It's good news for the healing, but it means we shall have to keep a close eye on him, lest he wanders about and further damages that leg. Right now, what he needs is—"

Wyatt stopped her by taking the broken pieces of the plate from her hand and setting them on the counter. Before she could say anything more, he gathered her up into his arms and held her. Whispering into her hair, he said, "Thank you. You've saved my son. I don't know what I would have done if you hadn't been there."

Julia's body warmed at his touch and she blushed. They were married and there was nothing wrong with such innocent touches as these, but she was so unaccustomed to them... and she had all but given up hope of ever experiencing them with Wyatt.

Biting her lip, she managed to answer, "He's my son, too, now, isn't he?"

Wyatt pulled away from her so that he could look her in the eyes, but his hands remained firmly on her shoulders. Slowly, a smile formed on his lips. It was a quiet, small smile, only noticeable because Julia had spent so much time watching how he frowned with those sweet lips. One of his hands lifted from her shoulder to push aside a strand of hair that had come loose from the high bun she had tied her golden curls into. He tucked it behind her ear, his finger caressing along her cheek at the same time.

"I never thought it was possible," he murmured quietly, staring at her as though he was in awe of her very presence. "I had loved my first wife so very much and I thought..." He shook his head. "I thought that it would be betrayal, a slight against her memory to ever feel in my heart again what I had felt for her." He placed a hand on his chest over where his heart would be. "But, Julia, I have lived with you for only a month, and you have wormed your way inside this old heart. It was your love for a boy who does not share your blood that proved to me that you are too good of a woman to lose."

Julia stared at him with wide eyes, her heart thumping loudly in her chest. The things he was saying to her she had believed were impossible. Her own heart had opened to him so quickly, but she had resigned herself to the realization that he would never feel the same. And now she dared to hope.

"What are you saying, Wyatt?" It was the first time she had spoken his first name aloud, and it settled sweetly on her tongue.

His eyes sparkled and his smile widened just a little bit. "I am saying that I have taken you already as my wife. Now, I am asking you to be my love."

Tears pricked at Julia's eyes and she could find no words to describe how she felt, so she threw her arms around his neck, hugging him tightly. His arms held her back and he promised her that he would take care of her for as long as she would have him.

It still took eight weeks for John's leg to heal and he was bedridden for all of them, but Julia entertained him with bright stories and his father brought all sorts of plants for him to squish between the pages of blank books. They grew together, leaning on each other for support, and by the end of it all, they were truly a happy family.

THE END

ABOUT THE AUTHOR

Charity Phillips grew up on a beautiful farm with her three brothers and two sisters in Cherokee County, North Carolina. She fell in love with horses and learned to care for them at an early age. She currently lives just a stone's throw from that gorgeous farm with her loving husband of twelve years and their three beautiful daughters. When Charity isn't dreaming up her next story, she's usually tending to her garden or baking delicious treats for her family.

To keep up to date with her latest releases, you may visit www.hopemeadowpublishing.com and sign up for her newsletter.

For a **FREE** sweet historical romance e-book, please sign up for Hope Meadow Publishing's newsletter at www.hopemeadowpublishing.com.

Made in the USA
Lexington, KY
04 July 2017